Shock the Monkey

By

James Capper

Copyright © 2023 James Capper

All rights reserved. No part of this publication may be reproduced, distributed, or transmitted in any form or by any means without the prior written permission of the author.

Dedication

I would like to dedicate my book to Peter Gabriel. For it was his song that inspired me.

Acknowledgement

I'd like to thank Lynne Jones, Athena Grant, Kevin Standfield, and the professionals at Times Ghostwriters – Anna Wilson, Elijah Smith, and June Dankei.

About the Author

A person of reason with a creative mind!

CONTENTS

Dedication i
Acknowledgement ii
About the Author iii
Chapter 1 1
Chapter 2 15
Chapter 3 23
Chapter 4 46
Chapter 5 62
Chapter 6 83
Chapter 7 103
Chapter 8 122
Chapter 9 139
Chapter 10 160
Chapter 11 176
Chapter 12 193
Chapter 13 208
Chapter 14 217
Chapter 15 241
Chapter 16 246

Chapter 1

The air was thick with the scent of disinfectant, but it did little to mask the underlying stench of sweat, fear, and despair. The walls, made of cold, grey concrete, seemed to absorb the flickering light from the dimly lit corridor, casting long shadows that danced along the narrow hallway. It was a place where hope seemed to wither and die, where the echoes of past mistakes reverberated in the hearts of those locked away.

Ian, a seasoned detective, found himself walking through this bleak environment, accompanied by Robert Taylor, Corrections Officer (C.O). The two men approached a steel door with a small window at the top. Curiosity tugged at Ian, compelling him to inquire about the room beyond. With a sense of unease, he asked Robert about the purpose of this ominous place.

Robert chuckled in response, urging Ian to keep moving, but not without divulging a disturbing truth.

"It's called the shock room, detective," Robert explained, a chilling grin etching its way onto his face. "We sometimes have to 'shock the monkey,' as we call it. You see, it's been two decades, and your friend Simon, known as the Monkey, still maintains his innocence."

Ian's heart skipped a beat, and a shiver raced down his spine. He had heard whispers of the shock room's existence, tales of prisoners subjected to electric shocks in an effort to extract confessions. However, witnessing it firsthand was an entirely different reality. He couldn't fathom the depths of despair and pain that awaited those unfortunate souls behind that steel door.

"Why resort to such measures?" Ian's voice resonated with stern disapproval.

Robert shrugged callously, his tone devoid of remorse. "It's a scare tactic, detective," he replied matter-of-factly. "Most of the time, the mere threat of the shock is enough to make prisoners confess. But for those who stubbornly refuse to cooperate, we bring them here."

Disgust surged within Ian, his face contorting with disbelief. "That's torture," he asserted firmly. "It's inhumane."

Unfazed, Robert responded with indifference. "It's just a part of the job," he stated dismissively. "Besides, it's not like we do it all the time. Just for the really tough cases."

Ian struggled to reconcile the images in his mind—the flickering lights, the chilling grins, and the prison cells they passed along the way. Behind each metal door, a person lived, trapped in a cycle of despair. Some paced relentlessly, their steps echoing their restless minds, while others sat motionless, their eyes hollow, fixated on the barren walls. The thunderous clang of the doors being slammed shut punctuated the air, a constant reminder of confinement.

In that moment, Ian was confronted with a moral dilemma. He knew, deep within his core, that justice could never be achieved through such cruel means. The blurred line between right and wrong, the pressure and challenges faced by those tasked with upholding the law—these factors played havoc with his conscience.

As they continued their somber journey down the corridor, Ian couldn't help but ponder the cost of justice in a world where darkness tainted the very institutions meant to protect society. The corridor stretched on, the shadows growing longer, as if whispering the secrets of those who had been forgotten within these unforgiving walls.

Detective Ian felt the weight of anticipation settling upon his shoulders as he sat in his chair, surrounded by the remnants of countless unsolved cases. The corridor leading to the interrogation room stretched out before him, seemingly endless, a haunting reminder of the void that awaited him. He knew that beyond that empty space lay a prisoner, a key to unlocking the secrets of the elusive bank robber known as 'The Monkey.'

The pen in his hand became an instrument of restless energy, tapping against the desk in sync with the rhythm of his racing thoughts. The details of the robbery swirled through his mind like a whirlwind, each piece of the puzzle demanding his attention. How had this enigmatic thief managed to escape unscathed, leaving behind only a trail of unanswered questions?

Beside him, Roni, his partner, combed through the case files with unwavering focus. The tension in the room was palpable as they delved deeper into the intricate web of clues and possibilities. The heist had the hallmarks of an inside job, a meticulously executed plan that required a level of expertise far beyond that of an ordinary criminal.

A flicker of intrigue danced in Ian's eyes as he took a sip of his coffee, the dark liquid fueling his determination. "The cameras were disabled manually," he mused, a faint smile touching his lips. It was a revelation that added another layer of complexity to the case. How had the culprit managed to disable the security cameras individually, circumventing the central security system? The audacity and meticulousness of the act hinted at a professional, someone with knowledge and experience beyond the ordinary thief.

Roni's brow furrowed, the weight of the situation etched on her face. "But how is that even possible?" she wondered aloud, rubbing her temple in an attempt to alleviate the rising frustration. The cameras were strategically positioned, placed at a considerable height that seemed almost insurmountable.

Ian leaned back in his chair, his mind working feverishly to connect the dots. "We're dealing with someone exceptional," he affirmed, the words carrying a mix of admiration and determination. This was no ordinary criminal; they were facing a formidable adversary, one who had carefully planned and executed their actions with meticulous precision.

The detectives locked eyes, their shared understanding cementing their resolve. They had embarked on a relentless pursuit of truth, determined to bring the perpetrator to justice and restore a sense of order in a world that had been thrown into disarray. It was a daunting task, but their unwavering dedication and unyielding spirit propelled them forward.

"We'll find him," Ian declared, his voice brimming with conviction. "We just have to keep digging, uncover every hidden detail, and follow the path that leads us to the truth. There's a clue out there waiting to be discovered."

And so, with renewed purpose, the two detectives dove back into the case files, their minds alight with possibility. They would interview witnesses, review security footage, and leave no stone unturned in their pursuit of justice. Their journey would take them to the bustling streets of Las Vegas, a city known for its secrets and intrigue, as they sought the elusive answers that lay hidden within its glittering façade.

As they sped down the open road, Ian's gaze fixed upon the horizon, his thoughts consumed by the tantalizing possibilities that awaited them. It was a race against time, a battle of wits, and Ian couldn't help but feel a sense of exhilaration coursing through his veins. The road ahead was paved with uncertainty, but in that uncertainty lay the promise of truth, justice, and the unmasking of 'The Monkey.'

Detective Ian's frustration simmered just beneath the surface as he contemplated the audacity of the thief they were pursuing. The brazenness of their actions, the precision with which they had bypassed the bank's security measures, left him in awe. This was no ordinary criminal, and their meticulous planning hinted at a mastermind behind the scenes.

"It's the third time in the past 6-months! I don't understand how he got away with so much money and unscathed, undetected!" Ian said, running his hand through his short, dark hair. "He had to have been planning this for months."

Roni nodded in agreement, her eyes scanning through the case files. "Probably someone from the inside. Maybe an employee or even a rogue security guard? It says here that he disabled the security cameras and took out the alarm system. That must have taken some serious expertise."

Ian's lips curled into a faint smile, his mind racing with possibilities. "But here's the intriguing part," he began, taking a deliberate sip of his coffee to savor the moment. "The cameras were not disabled through the central security system. They were disabled manually."

Roni's temple twitched as her mind grappled with the revelation. The security cameras, perched high above the ground, seemingly out of reach, had been meticulously tampered with by the cunning thief. The sheer audacity of such a feat left her momentarily dumbfounded.

"What?! Manually? How could he do that? There are more than a dozen security cameras in the bank, and they are placed at least 20 feet above the ground," Roni said, her temple throbbing as she tried to comprehend the audacity of the thief's actions.

Ian leaned back in his chair, deep in thought, contemplating the implications of the manual camera disablement. A faint smile played on his lips as a realization began to dawn upon him. "Yep! So it seems like we're dealing with a professional. This isn't just some random guy looking to make a quick buck."

Roni's frustration etched across her face, mirroring Ian's growing determination. "It's like he knew exactly what he was doing. How are we supposed to catch him?"

Ian shook his head, his gaze fixed on the files before him. "We'll find him. We just have to keep digging. There has to be a clue somewhere."

The two detectives continued poring over the case files, meticulously analyzing every detail. Their conversation ebbed and flowed as they brainstormed theories, dissected the evidence, and sought to unravel the enigma that surrounded 'The Monkey.'

During their investigation, a breakthrough occurred for Ian. He couldn't shake the feeling that something was amiss, as if a crucial detail had eluded their grasp. Lost in his train of thought, the missing puzzle piece finally fell into place.

"Pull over!" Ian exclaimed, breaking the silence, his voice filled with urgency.

"What? Here?" Roni asked, visibly perplexed.

"Do it!" Ian insisted, his mind racing with newfound clarity. Roni complied, and their car came to a halt on the desolate road, bathed only in the glow of the Cadillac's headlights.

"This is not the first time these robberies are happening," Ian began, his voice measured and determined. "Whoever is involved in these robberies is connected to similar cases of thefts that happened the same way back in 1970. And the person responsible for them is already serving life in prison."

Roni's confusion was evident as she sought to make sense of Ian's revelation. "Who?" she asked, her curiosity piqued.

"Can you pull out Simon's file for me?" Ian requested, his gaze fixed on the horizon.

Roni's eyes widened with disbelief. "Simon Grundfeld? Why do you want to see his file?"

Ian let out a heavy sigh. "Just pull it out, Roni. I need to look at it."

Complying with his request, Roni retrieved Simon Grundfeld's file and handed it to Ian. Opening it, Ian delved into the details of Simon's case, his eyes scanning the pages for any connection to the present-day bank robberies.

"In 1970, Simon was arrested for robbing a bank at night," Ian read aloud, his voice filled with intrigue. "The jury found him guilty and sentenced him to life without parole. For 20 years, Simon has professed his innocence, insisting that it was a case of mistaken identity. But all the evidence was against him."

Roni raised an eyebrow, her curiosity deepening. "What does this have to do with the bank robbery we're investigating?"

Ian closed the file, handing it back to Roni. A knowing smile tugged at the corners of his lips as he met her gaze. "Simon had multiple aliases. One of them was 'The Monkey.'"

Understanding washed over Roni's face as the pieces of the puzzle began to align. "So, you think Simon Grundfeld, the man serving life in prison, might have some connection to the recent bank robberies?"

Ian nodded, his eyes gleaming with a mix of determination and excitement. "Simon was known for his unique physical abilities, his agility, and his exceptional climbing skills. If anyone could disable the security cameras manually and execute these elaborate heists, it would be him."

Roni's face lit up with a mix of astonishment and anticipation. "What should we do now?"

A resolute look settled on Ian's face as he spoke with conviction. "We go back to L.A. We need to talk to Simon, 'The Monkey' himself."

Roni raised an eyebrow. "Again? What does this have to do with the bank robbery we're investigating?"

Ian closed the file and handed it back to Roni, his mind racing with a myriad of thoughts and suspicions. As the weight of their findings settled upon them, a suspenseful question hung in the air, creating an irresistible curiosity for what lay ahead:

How did Simon, a seemingly unassuming and physically unremarkable man, manage to execute such audacious heists, eluding capture and leaving no trace of his involvement?

The puzzle pieces were slowly falling into place, revealing a complex web of deceit and hidden abilities. Ian couldn't help but wonder about the untapped depths of Simon's cunning mind and the secrets he held within the confines of his prison cell.

With each passing moment, their anticipation grew, fueled by the burning desire to confront 'The Monkey' and unravel the truth that had remained concealed for decades. What hidden talents and carefully crafted plans had propelled Simon to the center of their investigation? And more importantly, what awaited them as they ventured into the heart of the prison to meet the enigmatic mastermind face-to-face?

The endless corridor stretched out before Ian, a metaphorical path that mirrored the endless possibilities and unanswered questions swirling within his mind. Determined and relentless, he strode forward, ready to uncover the truth, no matter the risks involved.

The stage was set for the next chapter in their relentless pursuit of justice, as Ian and Roni prepared to confront 'The Monkey' and delve deeper into the intricate tapestry of the Los Angeles bank robberies. Little did they know the dark secrets and unforeseen twists that awaited them in the depths of Simon's past, waiting to be unraveled as the truth gradually revealed itself.

As they ventured into the depths of the prison, facing the daunting challenge of interrogating a man who had eluded capture for years, Ian and Roni braced themselves for the unknown. The stage was set, and the next chapter would test their resolve, their wits, and their determination to bring 'The Monkey' to justice once and for all.

Chapter 2

As Detective Ian closed the file, a sense of anticipation filled the air. The story of Simon, the elusive criminal mastermind known as 'The Monkey,' had captivated their attention. The puzzle pieces were scattered before them, and they were determined to unravel the enigma that lay hidden within the shadows.

With a determined gaze, Ian locked eyes with Roni, his partner in the intricate dance of deduction, as they stepped out of the cell.

Veronica Smith, a.k.a Roni, a black female detective within the LAPD, was a beacon of hope, a symbol of unity, and an embodiment of the unwavering commitment to justice that defined the department. Her name echoed through the halls, her legacy etched in the hearts of those she had touched.

Roni's journey had been paved with countless sacrifices within the corridors of the LAPD. Her dedication to her craft was unmatched, honed through years of training and a relentless pursuit of excellence. She had witnessed the darkest corners of humanity and emerged with an unyielding resolve to make a difference.

Ian recognized the strength of their diversity, understanding that it was their unity that made the LAPD a formidable and loyal department.

Their minds synchronized seamlessly, fueled by an unwavering curiosity that burned brighter with each passing moment. They shared the understanding that to capture a thief as cunning as Simon, they had to delve into his mindset, anticipating his every move. With this insatiable curiosity driving them forward, Ian felt an urgent need to narrate their pursuit of Simon, fueled by a determination to finally apprehend him.

"Simon was a small man, almost unremarkable in his appearance," Ian explained, his voice filled with a mixture of fascination and intrigue. His eyes sparkled with a glimmer of understanding as he continued to unveil the enigmatic figure known as Simon, or more famously, 'The Monkey.'

"He stood no taller than five and a half feet, and his body was thin and wiry as if he had been stretched out like a piece of taffy," Ian elaborated, painting a vivid image of Simon's physical attributes. It was clear that his unassuming appearance had served as a deceptive cloak, concealing the true extent of his capabilities.

"But despite his diminutive size," Ian continued, his voice laced with awe, "Simon possessed impressive agility and strength that belied his appearance." The contrast between Simon's physical stature and his innate prowess was astonishing.

Ian's words took on a poetic quality as he delved deeper into the extraordinary talents possessed by this criminal mastermind. "He moved with a lithe grace that seemed almost impossible for someone his size," he said, his voice filled with admiration. "Like a cat, he was fluid and quick, effortlessly evading capture and slipping away from pursuers with ease."

But it was Simon's skill as a climber that truly set him apart. Ian's voice dropped to a hushed tone, emphasizing the air of mystery surrounding this aspect of Simon's abilities. "He was a skilled climber, bordering on the supernatural," Ian revealed, his voice tinged with various mixed expressions. "Scaling walls and buildings seemed effortless to him. His fingers and toes found purchase on even the smallest cracks and crevices, allowing him to ascend and descend with otherworldly grace."

Ian's eyebrows arched as he raised them, a silent question hanging in the air. He looked at Roni, seeking confirmation that she understood the significance of his description.

Through his narration, Ian had painted a vivid picture of Simon, the elusive 'Monkey.' A man who defied expectations, blending into the shadows with his unremarkable appearance while possessing the agility and climbing skills of a creature seemingly from another world.

Roni's face looked like she just had a Eureka moment. "What should we do now?"

"We go back to L.A.," Ian said, getting back inside the car.

The passing scenery blurred outside the car window as Ian leaned back his head on his seat, lost in his thoughts. The rhythmic hum of the engine filled the silence within the vehicle, providing a soothing backdrop to the intensity of their mission. As the miles ticked away, the weight of the investigation pressed upon Ian's shoulders, demanding answers, demanding progress.

His gaze fixed on the distant horizon; his mind navigated the twists and turns of their journey so far. The encounters with witnesses, the meticulous examination of evidence, and the endless pursuit of the truth had led them to this moment. The realization that Simon, the enigmatic criminal mastermind known as 'The Monkey,' held the key to unlocking the secrets that plagued their investigation lingered heavily in the air.

"I gotta talk to the monkey," Ian finally uttered, breaking the silence. His voice carried a mix of determination and intrigue. The mere thought of confronting Simon, peeling back the layers of his mind, sent a thrill down Ian's spine. He knew that in order to understand the depths of Simon's cunning, he had to engage directly with the source, and immerse himself in the mind of a criminal genius.

Roni shot him a puzzled glance. "What do you mean, talk to the monkey?"

Roni's eyes flickered with a mixture of confusion and curiosity as she cast a puzzled glance in Ian's direction. The question hung in the air, waiting to be answered, as the car continued to glide along the highway, carrying them closer to their destination.

Ian sighed heavily. "I mean Simon. Simon Grundfeld. I need to talk to him."

Roni shook her head. "Ian, he's been in prison for 20 years. What makes you think he can help us with this bank robbery case?"

Ian shrugged. "I don't know. Maybe he can't. But I have a feeling that there's more to this case than meets the eye. And Simon, he's been protesting his innocence for 20 years. That has to count for something."

Roni rolled her eyes. "Fine. But we're going to have to jump through a lot of hoops to get permission to talk to him."

Ian nodded. "I know. But it's worth a shot."

The gravity of his words settled between them, the weight of the task at hand sinking deeper into their consciousness. Ian knew that facing 'The Monkey' directly was a risk, an encounter that could expose them to the cunning and dangerous world of this criminal mastermind. But it was a risk he was willing to take.

As the car carried them closer to the labyrinth of shadows where 'The Monkey' lurked, the air inside the vehicle crackled with a shared understanding. They were entering a realm of uncertainty, where the line between hunter and hunted blurred, and the stakes escalated with each passing breath.

The road ahead beckoned, challenging them to unravel the enigma that was 'The Monkey.' Ian's eyes glimmered with a mix of determination and a touch of exhilaration, silently communicating to Roni that the time for action was drawing near. Together, they would delve into the depths of a criminal mind, hoping to emerge victorious and bring an end to the elusive reign of 'The Monkey.'

As Ian and Roni were on their way to Vegas, Ian's mind was consumed with thoughts of the ongoing case. However, a sudden realization struck him like a lightning bolt. If Simon was languishing in prison, then who could be behind the recent string of robberies, executed in the exact same style?

A mix of confusion, curiosity, and concern washed over Ian's face. "Could it be possible? Is there someone impersonating Simon, carrying out these crimes?" he muttered to himself, his voice tinged with a hint of disbelief. His heart raced, realizing the implications of this revelation. It was more than just a twist in the case; it was a potential web of deception and danger.

Ian couldn't let it go. He couldn't ignore the gnawing feeling that there was more to the story, that justice had yet to prevail. Determination fueled his actions as he redirected his path, abandoning his Vegas-bound journey for now. Simon's name echoed in his mind, intertwining with the mysterious figure responsible for the robberies.

"I need to confront Simon," Ian said to Roni with a resolute tone, the weight of his responsibility hanging heavy in the air. "Only he can help me unravel this enigma, shed light on the truth, and put an end to these crimes. Time is of the essence."

With renewed purpose, Ian set off towards the prison, his emotions a mixture of anticipation, anxiety, and a glimmer of hope that this unexpected turn would lead to the answers he sought.

Chapter 3

Throughout history, there have been people with high intelligence and IQ who have chosen a life of crime and have been able to outsmart the police and authorities. Their examples demonstrate that intelligence can be used for good or evil.

These smart robbers possess a keen understanding of human psychology, exploiting weaknesses and vulnerabilities to their advantage. They meticulously observe the patterns of their targets, identifying the opportune moments when security is at its most vulnerable, and alarms are least likely to be triggered.

With calculated precision, they navigate through intricate networks of surveillance systems, bypassing state-of-the-art security measures as if they were mere child's play. Their knowledge of cutting-edge technology grants them the power to manipulate electronic locks, disable alarms, and erase their digital footprints, leaving behind little evidence of their presence.

However, while these mad geniuses and gifted people may seem impressive, it's important to remember that the impact of their crimes can be devastating, leading to financial loss, emotional trauma, and physical harm to innocent people, which can be scary at times to deal with!

These criminal masterminds employ a network of skilled individuals, each with a specific role to play in the grand scheme of their heists. From hackers who breach firewalls and secure databases to precision drivers who maneuver getaway vehicles with breathtaking skill, every member of their team is handpicked for their expertise and unwavering loyalty.

These smart robbers are a breed apart, their criminal prowess admired even by those sworn to bring them to justice. The challenge they present to law enforcement is not merely a matter of apprehending criminals; it is a battle of wits, a test of investigative skills, and a clash between innovation and the relentless pursuit of truth.

But as they push the boundaries of what is possible, they also ignite the determination of dedicated detectives like Ian and Roni, who refuse to yield in their pursuit of justice. Each intricate heist carries the seeds of its own unraveling, leaving behind traces that, with careful observation and relentless investigation, can lead to the downfall of even the smartest of criminals.

The planning process is a meticulous endeavor, spanning weeks, if not months, as they meticulously gather intelligence, scout locations, and establish contingency plans for every conceivable scenario. They study blueprints, map escape routes, and simulate the heist repeatedly, refining their strategies to perfection.

The execution of the heist itself is a symphony of synchronized movements and split-second decision-making. Communication occurs through encrypted channels, using code names and intricate hand signals to relay information without arousing suspicion. The robbers move like shadows, appearing and disappearing with a sense of ethereal grace, leaving witnesses bewildered and law enforcement officers one step behind.

To cover their tracks, they employ sophisticated methods to launder stolen money, ensuring it enters the legitimate financial system undetected. Offshore accounts, shell companies, and complex transactions become their playground as they manipulate the global economy to their advantage.

And so, the cat-and-mouse game continues, with both sides locked in an ever-evolving dance of intellect and determination. The smart robbers leave their mark on history, their legends whispered in hushed tones, but they are never beyond the reach of those who strive to bring them to justice.

Los Angeles, the summer of 1990, months before Ian found himself in front of Simon's cell. The city was buzzing with activity, with its numerous beaches, amusement parks, and tourist attractions drawing in crowds of people from all over the world.

The city was known for its year-round sunshine, but in the summer months, the temperatures soared, making it the perfect time for locals and tourists alike to hit the beach. The Hollywood scene was still thriving, with big movie studios such as Paramount Pictures and Warner Bros. Pictures producing hit films. The city was home to many famous actors and musicians, including Michael Jackson, who was at the height of his career.

Despite the glamour and allure of Los Angeles, the city was not immune to its share of problems. Beneath the surface of its shimmering façade, crime lurked in the shadows, casting a dark cloud over the City of Angels.

Crime rates soared in certain neighborhoods, fueled by the presence of gangs, drug trafficking, and organized crime syndicates. The police force, already burdened with the task of protecting a sprawling metropolis, found themselves constantly stretched thin as they tried to keep up with the relentless tide of criminal activity.

The city's diverse population provided fertile ground for various forms of illicit activities. From back-alley deals to white-collar schemes, the underbelly of Los Angeles thrived, its web of corruption extending its tendrils into every corner of society.

It was a city of contradictions, where the bright lights of Hollywood and the beauty of its beaches were offset by the darker side of crime. The city of Angels was under siege, with a series of brazen robberies and murders sweeping across the city. The residents of Los Angeles were on edge, with fear gripping their hearts as they wondered when and where the next crime would occur.

The police were at their wits' end, struggling to keep up with the increasing number of crimes and robberies. The criminal who was responsible seemed to be one step ahead of them at every turn, leaving no clues behind and making his escapes without a trace.

At first, the police believed that these were isolated incidents, the work of small-time criminals looking to make it big. The initial assumption was that Los Angeles had fallen victim to a wave of opportunistic robberies and murders, each case seemingly unconnected. However, as the evidence accumulated and the puzzle pieces began to align, a troubling realization set in: they were dealing with something far more sinister than they had originally thought.

It was evident that a criminal mastermind was at work, meticulously orchestrating a series of robberies and murders with surgical precision. This was no ordinary criminal but someone who possessed a profound understanding of the criminal underworld and the intricacies of executing complex crimes.

As the investigation unfolded, law enforcement agencies found themselves grappling with the realization that they were dealing with a highly intelligent and calculated individual. This criminal operated in the shadows, leaving behind minimal evidence and expertly covering their tracks. Their knowledge of security systems, their ability to exploit weaknesses, and their knack for eluding capture suggested a level of expertise acquired through years of experience.

The scale and audacity of the crimes sent shockwaves through the city. The targets were carefully selected, indicating a deep understanding of their vulnerabilities and potential gains. The robberies were executed swiftly and efficiently, leaving little room for error. In each case, the criminal left no witnesses and vanished without a trace, frustrating the authorities, who were desperate for leads.

The police started to piece together the clues, studying the modus operandi of the criminal and the patterns that emerged from his actions.

The criminal's ability to stay one step ahead of the authorities created an air of uncertainty and unease. Detectives and investigators worked tirelessly to decipher the intricate web of connections, searching for any clues that would lead them closer to unraveling the identity of the Mastermind. But with each new lead, the criminal seemed to anticipate their moves, sidestepping capture and leaving behind only a trail of perplexing puzzles.

With each passing day, the stakes grew higher, and the urgency to apprehend the Mastermind intensified. The city yearned for an end to the reign of terror and the restoration of peace. The criminal's shadow loomed large over Los Angeles, a constant reminder of their ability to outwit and outmaneuver those who sought to stop them.

But the mastermind was smart, using advanced tactics to evade the police's surveillance systems and covering his tracks with meticulous care. He left no fingerprints, no DNA, and no traces of evidence, making it almost impossible for the police to catch him.

Despite their best efforts, the police were unable to make any headway in the case. They were frustrated and demoralized, with the realization sinking in that they were dealing with a criminal who was far superior to their abilities.

The criminal continued to wreak havoc across the city, striking at will and with impunity. He was targeting high-value targets, such as businessmen, banks, jewelry stores, museums, and luxury homes, making off with millions of dollars in cash and valuables and leaving a trail of dead bodies behind.

The city was in chaos, with people living in constant fear of becoming the next victim. The authorities knew they had to act fast, and they decided to bring in the best minds in law enforcement to help them crack the case. They enlisted the help of the FBI, the DEA, and other federal agencies, hoping to pool their resources and expertise to catch the elusive criminal mastermind.

District Attorney Samantha Williams was headstrong in catching this criminal mastermind and had put the best detectives in her unit, Ian Fisk and Roni, on this case.

Samantha Williams was a renowned district attorney and her office had its own investigators. The detectives from her office handled investigative details that weren't addressed in the police investigation, and occasionally investigations of public officers where the police department might be handicapped by politics in handling the investigation.

Ian and Roni were former police detectives who established a great record of work. It would be very unusual for someone to be appointed to one of the position of D.A right out of college or out of the police academy. Ian was first appointed as a police officer and from there he worked his way into an investigative slot, then convinced Samantha that he was a good enough candidate to be appointed to the DA investigators corps.

The role of detectives in a DA investigator corps was to flesh out investigations that were usually started by patrol officers. When the investigation was complete, they presented it to the district attorney for charge. The district attorney made the decision and took it from there.

Once in a while, some district attorney offices want to get in on the investigation from the very start until the final conclusion. They want to make sure that all of the legal requirements are handled as professionally as possible. Being lawyers and prosecutors in these cases, they present a different and valuable perspective that helps make sure that the investigation proceeds within the boundaries of the law.

Being appointed by the influential and strict D.A Samantha was, Ian and Roni left no stones unturned as they poured over surveillance footage, studied the movements of the criminal, and analyzed every piece of data they could find.

Despite their efforts, progress was slow, with the assailant staying one step ahead at every turn. It seemed that the more they investigated, the more the criminal learned about their methods and tactics.

Crime scenes have a way of captivating the imagination, each one telling a story of its own. Some crimes, however, possess an intricate complexity that leaves even seasoned investigators scratching their heads.

Detective Ian and Detective Roni found themselves in one such perplexing scenario, standing alongside the Police Chief, their eyes fixed upon the lifeless body of Troy Henson, a wealthy billionaire whose existence had been abruptly extinguished.

The room in which they stood bore the chaotic aftermath of a struggle, a battleground of overturned furniture and scattered documents. The safe, once a symbol of impenetrable security, now stood open and devoid of its valuable contents. It was a scene that spoke of meticulous planning and mastery of deception.

Ian's keen eyes scanned the room, piecing together the puzzle before him. "Looks like a professional job," he remarked, his voice laden with a mix of intrigue and frustration. The precision displayed in the execution of the crime left little doubt in his mind.

Roni, her analytical mind ever at work, voiced the question that hung heavy in the air. "But how did they gain entry? The door was locked from the inside, and there are no signs of forced entry."

The Police Chief nodded in agreement, his gaze fixed upon the lifeless body before them. "Indeed, that's the million-dollar question. Whoever orchestrated this heinous act possessed an intimate understanding of security protocols, leaving behind no trace of their method of entry."

Ian's pen moved swiftly across the pages of his notebook, capturing the details that would serve as fragments of truth in an enigmatic puzzle. "Could it have been an inside job? Someone among the security guards or a member of Henson's staff?"

The Police Chief dismissed the notion with a solemn shake of his head. "We have already scrutinized every person connected to Henson's inner circle. Alibis were verified, and meticulous checks were conducted on their communication records and surveillance footage. Henson was not a saint, he had cases pending against him in the court of law but no one within his immediate circle appears to have played a role in this crime."

Furrowing his brow, Ian was determined to uncover the elusive truth. "If the killer had not received assistance from within, then how did they bypass the layers of security undetected?"

Silence hung heavy in the room as the trio contemplated the possibilities, their minds racing to unravel the intricacies of the crime. Their attention gravitated towards the formidable safe, its advanced security features now rendered futile in the face of the unknown assailant.

Roni leaned in closer, her eyes narrowing in on the intricate mechanisms that guarded the secrets within. "Do you think the perpetrator had a confidant? Someone with insider knowledge, capable of circumventing these sophisticated security measures?"

The Police Chief weighed the notion carefully, his expression betraying the weight of his responsibility. "It is a possibility we cannot dismiss. We shall revisit our inquiries, delving deeper into the lives of those connected to Henson, observing their behavior for the smallest hint of a slip."

With the weight of the investigation pressing upon them, Ian, Roni, and the Police Chief knew that time was of the essence. The puzzle before them demanded their unwavering dedication and resourcefulness. They would unravel the secrets concealed within the crime scene, peeling back the layers of deception and deceit until the truth was exposed and justice could prevail.

The path forward was uncertain, but their resolve burned brightly, fueled by a relentless pursuit of answers. In a city where appearances often masked sinister intentions, the detectives would leave no stone unturned, for they understood that every clue, every conversation, held the potential to bring them closer to the enigma that lurked in the shadows, waiting to be unmasked.

As the crime scene continued to unfold its enigmatic secrets, a sense of urgency hung heavy in the air. Just as the detectives contemplated their next move, a crime scene technician approached the trio, bearing news that demanded their immediate attention. The Police Chief, Ian, and Roni followed the technician to a separate room, their curiosity piqued by the discovery that awaited them.

A computer screen illuminated the dimly lit room, displaying footage from one of the security cameras. Their eyes widened in astonishment as the image played before them, revealing a figure materializing seemingly out of thin air. The room fell into stunned silence, broken only by the hushed whisper of the Police Chief, his voice barely audible, "That's impossible."

Ian exchanged a solemn glance with Roni, the weight of their realization settling upon them. "Looks like we're dealing with someone who possesses the ability to vanish without a trace," he stated, his tone reflecting both the challenge and determination that lay ahead. The need to identify and apprehend this elusive individual had taken on an even greater urgency.

In the midst of their contemplation, Ian and Roni were approached by a fellow officer, bearing urgent news from Samantha Williams, the District Attorney. Any development in the case demanded their immediate attention, prompting the detectives to make their way to her office.

As they entered the D.A. office, Samantha sat behind her desk, surrounded by a sea of case files. Her blonde hair cascaded flawlessly around her face, her piercing gaze conveying a steely resolve. It was clear that she, too, understood the gravity of the situation.

Ian and Roni took their seats, their attention fixated on Samantha as she spoke, her voice unwavering. "Ian, Roni, we've been tirelessly working on this case for months, but we've hit a roadblock. We need a breakthrough."

Ian's inquisitive nature prompted him to inquire further.

"What do you have in mind? How can we make progress?"

Samantha leaned forward, her expression serious. "I have an informer in Las Vegas who might possess crucial information regarding the elusive criminal we're up against. I need you two to go meet him and see what he knows."

A glimmer of intrigue sparkled in Ian's eyes as he absorbed the gravity of the situation. "Who is this informer, Samantha? Can we trust him?"

Samantha's response carried the weight of assurance. "He has proven himself to be a reliable source in the past, providing valuable insights in numerous high-profile cases. While I can't disclose his true identity for his own safety, I assure you, he is trustworthy."

Ian and Roni exchanged a silent exchange of determination, a shared commitment to bring an end to the relentless criminal who had eluded them for far too long. Troy Henson's tragic demise demanded justice, and they were prepared to go to great lengths to ensure it was served.

Ian hesitated for a moment, feeling a sense of unease. He had a gut feeling that something was off about this informer, but he couldn't put his finger on what it was. He looked over at Roni, who seemed to be weighing the options as well.

"We'll do it," Ian said finally, his decision made. "When do we leave?"

"As soon as possible. I'll arrange for your travel and accommodations in Las Vegas. You'll meet the informer at a secure location, and I'll provide you with all the details you need," Samantha replied.

Ian nodded, a sense of trepidation settling in the pit of his stomach. He knew that they were taking a risk by relying on an informer, but he also knew that they needed a break in the case. He trusted Samantha's judgment, but he couldn't shake the feeling that something wasn't right.

Samantha kept looking at Ian with her eyes not leaving him and dialed a number and turned on the speaker. "I want you to talk to him before you go."

Ian shot a look at Roni, who was looking at him with a puzzled look.

"Detective Ian, what can you tell us?" he said, cutting to the chase.

"Henson's murder, right?" he said, his voice low and gravelly.

Ian and Roni exchanged a glance, and Ian spoke up. "Yes, that's correct. Do you have any information for us?"

The informer took a deep breath, his voice lowering even further. "I have information, but it's going to cost you. I want complete immunity and I want to be relocated to a different state with a new identity."

Ian felt his suspicions growing. This was starting to sound like a shakedown. "We can't just grant you immunity without any concrete information. What do you have for us?"

The informer said with a sly smile playing in his tone. "I have proof that the guy you are looking for is actually, drum roll, please... a police officer! He's been using his position to cover up his crimes and avoid suspicion. I have evidence that he's been involved in the murders of several high-profile individuals."

Ian felt a jolt of shock run through him. If what the informer was saying was true, it could blow the case wide open. But he couldn't help but feel skeptical. It seemed too convenient, too easy.

"What kind of evidence do you have?" Roni asked, her tone cautious.

"If you agree to my terms, then I will hand myself over to you. Come get me and get the evidence too. I do not want to spill the beans on a call and then get my guts spilled in a dark alley just because I did not close the deal, right, you feelin' me?" he said. The informer was being reasonable. He was scared for his life and doing this because he needed protection.

"All right, we will stay in touch," Ian said and hung up.

Ian pondered for a moment before responding, "All right, we'll go to Vegas, but I'm keeping my eyes open and my guard up."

Samantha nodded, "I understand your concern, Detective. That's why I want you to be extra careful."

"I'll make sure of it," Ian promised.

Samantha handed Ian a piece of paper with the informer's details. "His name is Jack Dill, and he's been a reliable source for us in the past. He's waiting for you at a hotel in Vegas. Be there tomorrow, and he'll give you the information you need."

Ian took the paper and thanked Samantha before heading out with Roni.

As they embarked on the journey back to the police station, the weight of their impending meeting with the informer bore heavily on Ian's mind. Doubt gnawed at him, causing a sense of unease to settle deep within his core. There was something peculiar about the entire situation, a niggling suspicion that refused to be ignored. The urgency displayed by the District Attorney, Samantha, coupled with the timing of the meeting, raised a red flag in Ian's investigative instincts.

Roni, ever perceptive of Ian's unease, broke the silence that hung between them. Her voice laced with curiosity, she asked, "You think something's fishy, Ian?"

Ian's eyes met Roni's, his expression a mixture of concern and determination. He nodded in response, the weight of his suspicions reflected in his furrowed brow. "Yeah, Roni, I do. But we can't afford to ignore it. We have to proceed with caution and see what this informer has to say."

Acknowledging the gravity of their mission, Ian's mind shifted to the practicalities of their upcoming journey. "Samantha has made the necessary arrangements for our flight," he mentioned, his voice tinged with a hint of resignation. The inevitability of their departure settled upon him, as if fate itself had conspired to lead them to this pivotal moment.

Roni's eyes sparkled with mischief, a mischievous grin spreading across her face. She glanced at Ian before playfully slapping the side of her Cadillac, her voice filled with excitement. "Nah, Chief, if we're heading to Vegas, we're going in style."

Ian couldn't help but chuckle at Roni's spirited remark, a brief respite from the weighty atmosphere that enveloped them. As the engine roared to life, the Cadillac became a symbol of their resilience and determination, ready to whisk them away to the enigmatic city of Las Vegas. Their pursuit of the truth, guided by the shadows of doubt, would now unfold amidst the glitz and glamour of a city known for its secrets and allure.

With the wind against their faces and the road stretching out before them, Ian and Roni embarked on their journey, armed with a mixture of anticipation and caution. The twists and turns that lay ahead would test their mettle, but the desire for justice burned brightly within their hearts. In the face of uncertainty, they would rely on their partnership and the unyielding pursuit of truth as they delved into the heart of the city that never slept.

Chapter 4

Ian and Roni had big plans for the informer in Vegas, but their sudden realization upon Ian that Simon might know something about the case made them come back to Los Angeles.

And here he was with just a door standing in between the culprit and him. As Detective Ian descended the creaky wooden steps, the sound echoed eerily throughout the dimly lit cellar. The air grew thicker, suffused with a musty odor that permeated the space, making it difficult for him to breathe. The oppressive atmosphere seemed to bear the weight of countless secrets hidden within its walls, each brick whispering tales of illicit activities and unsolved mysteries.

Detective Ian took a moment to steady himself, his mind racing with anticipation and the weight of the investigation. He knew that opening this door would reveal a pivotal moment in the case, potentially exposing the secrets that had eluded him thus far. The realization that the informer in Vegas might hold critical information intensified his resolve, fueling a mix of anxiety and determination.

The chilling presence of confinement hung heavy in the atmosphere as the door opened, and he went inside. The Robert stationed at the entrance, a seasoned officer known for his dark humor, couldn't resist a jest as Ian passed by.

"Knock yourself out, Detective," Robert chuckled, the corners of his mouth curling up mischievously. Ian offered a nod in response, his focus was unwavering as he prepared to face the man confined within.

The stifling silence of the cellar seemed to press down on Detective Ian, amplifying the tension in the room. He took a step forward, cautiously closing the distance between himself and Simon, aware that every word and gesture could hold the key to unlocking the truth.

Detective Ian's gaze fell upon Simon, the man known as "the Monkey."

As Simon sat on a worn-out bed, his body language portrayed years of isolation. He was scribbling furiously in a journal, lost in his thoughts until Ian's arrival caught his attention.

"Simon," Ian spoke softly, his voice cutting through the heavy air. "We need to talk. We know you've been involved in some shady dealings, and we believe you might have information that can help us solve a case."

The dim light casts a haunting shadow over his figure, emphasizing his lanky and thin frame. It was as if years of isolation had drained every ounce of vitality from his being, leaving behind a mere shell of a man.

Simon's eyes, dull and weary, met Ian's gaze for a brief moment before darting away. He closed his journal with a deliberate motion as if guarding his thoughts from prying eyes. The dim light cast unsettling shadows across his face, revealing lines of weariness etched deeply into his features.

As he turned to look at him, Simon's features struck Ian as peculiar, something primal lingering within them. There was a rawness, a primitiveness that emanated from his countenance. It was as if the weight of his confinement had regressed him to a more primitive state, eroding the veneer of civilization.

His eyes, once bright and filled with life, now held a distant, haunted look. The flickering lights reflected in them, revealing a glimmer of sadness and desperation that seemed etched into the depths of his soul. They were windows to a tortured existence, windows that had witnessed unspeakable horrors.

Simon's face bore the marks of time and anguish. Deep lines etched across his forehead and around his eyes, evidence of the weight he had carried for far too long. His cheeks, once filled with youthful vitality, now seemed hollow, as if the years of solitude had sucked away every ounce of vitality.

The contours of his face held a certain asymmetry as if nature itself had shaped him with a touch of indifference. His nose, slightly crooked, hinted at past encounters with violence and hardship. His lips, cracked and dry, betrayed a lack of care, a neglect that had become his constant companion. But wait! Was it really true? Or Ian would now discover the reason behind him being MONKEY!

As Ian observed Simon, he couldn't help but feel a tinge of sympathy deep within his heart. This man, once a living, breathing and accomplished soul, had been reduced to mere existence in the depths of the cellar. He was the President of a renowned bank once but the world had forgotten him, locked him away for committing robbery in his own bank, and the toll it had taken on his spirit was painfully evident. All of his respect and security for his future was lost in a jiff.

The nickname "the Monkey" suddenly made sense to Ian. It wasn't just a moniker derived from his agility or cunning. It was a reflection of the primal nature that lingered within Simon's very essence, a connection to a part of humanity that lay dormant within each of us.

In that moment, Ian's eyes met Simon's, and he saw a flicker of recognition, a glimmer of the humanity that still lingered within him. Despite the hardened exterior, there was a vulnerability, a longing for connection that permeated his gaze.

Detective Ian couldn't help but wonder about the life Simon had lived before he became a prisoner of his own making. What circumstances had shaped him into the person he was today? What demons had haunted his past, driving him to commit acts that would forever brand him as a criminal? Too many questions queued his mind, and he had the answer to none!

The weight of the truth, the complexity of Simon's existence, weighed heavily on Ian's shoulders. In that cellar, surrounded by the echoes of darkness, he saw a man who had been cast aside by society, left to wither away in the depths of his own despair.

Simon's face broke into a weary and eerie smile as Ian approached him. "Welcome to my humble abode," he greeted Ian, his voice carrying a hint of both desperation and resignation. "I wish I could offer you something, but as you can see, there is nothing but insects and mice here with me for the past twenty fuckin' years!"

He punctuated his words by hurling the steel tray lying next to him on the bed with stale food to the wall. The sound reverberated in the air, an echo of his anguish. Tears welled up in his eyes, and he hastily wiped them away, apologizing for his emotional outburst.

"I'm sorry," Simon said, his voice trembling with pent-up emotions. "It's been years since someone came to see me. The loneliness can drive a man to the edge of his sanity."

Ian took in the scene, a mixture of pity and curiosity swirling within him. He had studied the case extensively, the ingenious acts of crime committed by Simon still fresh in his mind. But face-to-face with the man now, the lines between perpetrator and victim blurred, revealing a complex web of humanity and despair.

Pushing aside his conflicting emotions, Ian maintained his professional demeanor. "I'm here to interrogate you, Simon," he stated, his tone firm yet tinged with empathy. "I was on my way to Vegas to interrogate an informer. Trust me, no one would pass a chance to enjoy a weekend at the department's expense in Vegas, but I came back from halfway because I believe you are the key to the case I am investigating. I can end your misery if you can help me. There are still unanswered questions that need to be addressed."

Simon's smile faltered, his eyes clouding with a mix of anxiety and apprehension. He closed his journal with a thud, setting it aside, and looked directly into Ian's eyes. "I understand," he replied, his voice tinged with resignation. "Ask me anything you want. Try your luck. I have nothing left to hide. Twenty years is a lot, Detective. If there was something, I would have already told someone." With this, he smirked.

Ian took a moment to observe Simon, noticing the subtle lines etched on his face and the weariness in his eyes. It was a face that had witnessed unspeakable horrors and had borne the weight of guilt and regret for far too long.

"I need to know how?" Ian said, his voice softened. "How did you commit those acts? How is your gang or accomplice still operating?"

Simon's gaze faltered, his eyes dropping to the floor. He took a deep breath before answering, his voice laden with remorse. "I can't justify what I've done. There's no excuse for the pain I've caused. The crimes that happened were very real, and I feel the utmost sympathy for the people who were affected. It is just that I DID NOT FUCKING DO IT!" he yelled, his voice ringing in the cellar. "You think I like being like this? I have asked them to euthanize me! In the depths of my isolation, my mind has become a prison. I lost touch with reality, consumed by the demons within."

Ian nodded; he kept himself to calmest, his gaze unwavering. He had encountered many criminals throughout his career, each with their own twisted motivations. But Simon's case felt different, more tragic. There was a brokenness within him, a man who had descended into darkness and was now grappling with the consequences of actions he said he did not commit.

"I understand," Ian said, his voice gentle. "But there were people who cared about you, people who could have helped. Why didn't you reach out to them?"

Simon's expression shifted, a flicker of anger crossing his face. "You don't understand," he spat out, his voice rising. "I tried, I begged for help, but no one listened. They all turned a blind eye, and I was left to rot in this hellhole. No one believed me."

"Now, it's you sittin' here, trying to interrogate me! To hell with your investigation!" Simon angrily continued, pointing his finger at Ian.

But Ian wasn't ready to believe that Simon was innocent. He had full control of his temper and actions.

Ian leaned in, his eyes fixed on Simon. "Who did you reach out to? Who ignored your pleas for help?"

Simon's jaw clenched, his eyes burning with resentment. "It doesn't matter," he said, his voice cold. "It's too late now."

Ian persisted, his voice unwavering. "It does matter, Simon. If there's someone out there who could have prevented this, or someone who needs to be held accountable, now is the time."

Simon's eyes narrowed, his expression guarded. "It was my family, my friends, my employer," he said, his voice barely audible. "They couldn't handle the shame, the disgrace. They threw me away, and I was left to rot in this cellar."

Ian felt a pang of sympathy, the weight of Simon's words heavy on his shoulders. He knew all too well the destructive power of shame and fear, the toxic combination that could tear families apart.

"Simon," Ian began, his voice filled with compassion, "I know that life hasn't been kind to you. But we believe you have vital information that can help us bring justice to those who have been wronged. Please, trust us and share what you know."

Simon's gaze shifted, a mix of defiance and resignation. "Why should I trust you? The world has turned its back on me. I've been forgotten, discarded like trash."

"I'm sorry, Simon," Ian said, his voice softening. "I'm really sorry that you had to endure this alone. But you have to understand that what happened was wrong, and all the evidence pointed toward you. The surveillance footage and witnesses. If there was someone else, if there was another name, you could have told us, but you did not, and here we are."

Simon nodded, his eyes downcast. "I know," he said, his voice resigned. "You are barking at the wrong tree, detective. This corrupt and incompetent system does not care about justice. They just want to solve the case, and if they believe I am the culprit, I'm ready to face whatever punishment awaits me."

Ian stood up, his gaze lingering on Simon for a moment. He felt a sense of sadness, a man who had lost everything, his sanity, his freedom, and his family. But he also felt a sense of duty, a responsibility to ensure that justice was served.

"Simon, it is happening again. The crimes. Just the way you did it. Same precision and stealth. It could not be anyone else, but this time there was a trail of bodies. People are dying, Simon. This is your time to redeem yourself. Take a name!" Ian said his voice firm. "There are still procedures to follow, but I promise you, I'll make sure that your story is heard," Ian said, then paused.

"You know how serious the situation is! I want your full co-operation. People are dying!" He continued with an urgency in his tone.

Simon sat there for a moment, lost in thought, his mind racing with memories and regrets. He picked up his journal, flipping through the pages, the words etched on the paper a testament to his pain and loneliness.

"My story? They showed my face all over the news. Story of how I robbed people of millions of dollars while my family suffered in poverty while the only breadwinner of the house rotted and got abused in jail. My family was shamed! Is that how you are planning to do it all again?!" Simon spat.

Ian leaned back, his brows furrowing in contemplation. He had spent months poring over the case files, studying every detail meticulously. The evidence seemed solid, but there was a glimmer of doubt in Simon's eyes, a conviction in his voice that made Ian question his own certainty.

"I understand that you're denying these allegations," Ian replied, his tone measured. "But the evidence against you was substantial. You know that too! We can't simply ignore it. If you didn't do it, then who did? Who was he? Are you trying to cover for him when he left you here rotting for the rest of your life?" Ian said, trying to make his point valid for Simon.

Simon's lips curled into a cynical smile, his laughter echoing through the cellar. It was like nothing made any difference to him. The sound was filled with bitterness and desperation, a man at the end of his rope. "Oh, Detective, if I knew who did it, don't you think I would have said so by now? I've been rotting in this cellar for two decades; I've been cut off from the world, from any information. How am I supposed to know whose behind these crimes?"

Ian's frustration grew as he listened to Simon's words. The case seemed to be slipping further away from him, the truth elusive in the darkness of the cellar. He clenched his fists, his determination unwavering.

"Simon, we need your cooperation," Ian implored, his voice tinged with urgency. "If you truly didn't commit those robberies, help us find the real culprits. Help us bring justice to the victims. Help us bring justice to you."

Simon's laughter turned hollow, a tinge of madness seeping through. "Justice? You talk about justice while I've been locked away like an animal for crimes I didn't commit," he retorted, his voice rising. "What justice is there for me?"

Ian leaned forward, his eyes locked on Simon's. "Justice isn't just about punishment, Simon. You need to understand this. It's about finding the truth, about righting the wrongs. If you're innocent, then we need to uncover the real culprits, no matter the cost."

"If we don't catch the culprit on time, the crimes will continue to go, and there will be no safe place for people to go! You get my point?" Ian politely said.

Simon's expression hardened, his eyes narrowing. "And what about the cost to me? What about the years I've lost, the life that's been stolen from me? How do you propose to compensate for that?"

Ian's voice softened, his empathy seeping through his professional facade. "I can't give you back the years you've lost, Simon. But I can promise you that I will do everything in my power to uncover the truth. We'll re-examine the evidence, follow new leads, and find the real perpetrators. You have my word."

"FUCK YOU! I have heard that one before," Simon said, scribbling on his journal without even looking at Ian. That was the end of the road for the interrogation.

"Suit yourself. I will be back soon, Simon. Make up your mind," Ian said as he got up and asked Robert to open the door. The door opened, and as Ian walked away from the cellar, he heard a distant shout, "I DID NOT DO IT!"

After the intense interrogation with Simon, Detective Ian was determined to delve deeper into the enigma surrounding the criminal's past. He returned to the precinct, filled with a sense of urgency, eager to uncover any information that could shed light on Simon's aliases or previous activities.

Ian rummaged through the dusty archives, poring over old case files, searching for any clues that might connect to Simon's past. He flipped through faded photographs, scanned handwritten reports, and meticulously examined every document that could hold a piece of the puzzle.

Hours turned into days as Ian immersed himself in the search fueled by a relentless desire to unearth the truth. But despite his best efforts, he found himself hitting a dead end. The archives offered no substantial leads, no evidence of the aliases Simon might have used.

Frustration mounted within Ian as he contemplated the possibility that Simon had operated under a shroud of secrecy, leaving behind no trace of his past activities. It seemed as if the criminal had slipped through the cracks, erasing any remnants of his former identity.

Ian leaned back in his chair, a mixture of disappointment and exhaustion washing over him. He had hoped to find some tangible thread, a connection that would help piece together the scattered fragments of Simon's past. But all he had were empty pages, void of the answers he sought.

A glimmer of doubt flickered in Ian's mind. Had he been chasing a ghost all along? Was Simon truly a master of deception, or was there a possibility that the truth was buried deeper than he could fathom?

Chapter 5

With a sigh, Ian closed the last file and stared at the blank wall before him. He felt a sense of defeat, a recognition that the road ahead would be far more confusing than he had anticipated. Simon had proven to be a cunning person, an elusive figure who had managed to evade detection for decades.

But Ian was not one to give up easily. The setback only fueled his determination to explore other avenues. Perhaps there were witnesses who could shed light on Simon's activities, individuals who had encountered him during his criminal endeavors. It was time to dig deeper into the shadows, to seek out those who might hold the key to unraveling the mysteries surrounding Simon's past.

Ian had his mind focused on the next steps. He would reach out to the informer D.A. Samantha told him about, re-interview old associates, and explore any leads, no matter how faint they might be. He knew that the truth was out there, waiting to be discovered, and he was resolved to find it.

To work on Samantha's advice, Ian decided to visit the police station. Detective Ian's footsteps echoed through the corridors of the station as he made his way toward the archives. He was ready to spend countless hours poring over case files, witness statements, and evidence, but one name continued to haunt him—Simon, the elusive figure who had eluded justice for far too long. A single clue could be a game-changer for him!

As he entered the archives, the scent of aged paper and dust filled the air, creating an atmosphere of nostalgia and hidden secrets. Ian approached the rows of neatly organized file cabinets, their contents holding the potential to shed light on Simon's aliases and connections.

With meticulous care, he began his search, pulling out file after file, each one representing a glimpse into a different facet of the criminal underworld. Ian's eyes scanned the pages, his mind working overtime to detect any patterns or leads that might point him in the right direction.

Hours turned into days as Ian immersed himself in the world of Simon's aliases. He unearthed connections to various criminal enterprises, tracing a web of deceit and manipulation that spanned years. The deeper he delved, the more he realized the extent of the danger that lay ahead.

But amidst the chaos and complexity, a glimmer of hope emerged. Ian discovered an informer, code-named "Whisper," who had once crossed paths with Simon. The informer had vanished into the shadows years ago, but their knowledge could prove invaluable in cracking the case.

"He was a skilled hacker, capable of navigating the darkest corners of the digital world," Roni explained, her voice tinged with a mix of caution and excitement.

Roni had worked on a case before where she had to study and learn about 'Whisper' who hacked a banks mainframe and gave them a run for their money. When Ian mentioned 'Whisper' to Roni, she picked up from where she left last time.

"Whisper had contacts within the criminal underworld and a knack for uncovering secrets. But one day, he vanished, leaving behind only whispers of his existence."

Ian leaned forward, captivated by Roni's words. "Do you think he could be the missing link in our investigation?"

Roni nodded. "It's possible. Whisper had a reputation for being elusive, just like Simon. If anyone knows the truth about his whereabouts and activities, it would be him."

With newfound hope, Ian and Roni began the painstaking process of tracking down the elusive Whisper. They revisited old case files, re-interviewed witnesses, and used their network of contacts to gather information. Each lead, no matter how faint, brought them closer to uncovering the whereabouts of the mysterious informer.

Their efforts eventually paid off when they received a tip about a hidden underground network known as "The Haven." Rumors had it that Whisper frequented this covert gathering place, where individuals with valuable information exchanged secrets for protection.

Detective Ian and Roni sat in their dimly lit office, surrounded by stacks of files and a map with pins marking various locations. They were not new to this game of cat and mouse. They were skilled in infiltrating gatherings where people from the law were unwanted.

"The Haven" was not a place, it rather was an event that was held every month. It was where all the criminals, murderers, smugglers on the top of the criminal underworld food chain would gather and would exchange information and made all kinds of deals.

"Another one of these gatherings, huh? It feels like we're always chasing shadows in these circles" Ian said leaning back in his chair.

"Well, boss, that's where the real action happens. We need to be where the law can't reach, among the criminals themselves. It's the only way we'll get the information we need", Roni said smirking.

"You're right, Roni. We've been down this road before. Let's hope this time we find the answers we're looking for" Ian said nodding and lighting up a cigarette.

Roni picked up her phone and began making calls, her fingers tapping on the keypad with precision. After a few hours of relentless investigation, she finally uncovered the location they sought.

"All right, boss. There is this villa in the middle of the Nevada desert, nestled between the mountains. That's where "The Haven" will be held. I have the coordinates right here.

It's a masquerade party, and we'll be using fake names too" Roni said briefing Ian.

"A masquerade party? Well, well. That adds a bit of flair to our mission, doesn't it?" Ian said perking up.

"Indeed, boss. We'll have to play the part if we want to gain their trust and get close to Whisper" Roni said.

"Whisper, huh? That's a dangerous game we're playing. He's is virtually invisible and no one has ever even seen his face. What do we know about them? We do not even know his name" Ian said rubbing his forehead.

"Not much, boss. That's why we need to attend "The Haven" and see what information we can dig up. He would be in the basement at the tech hub. He will find us. He probably know by now that we are looking for him and at Haven he knows we cannot touch him. He will never miss an opportunity to do a deal or make a connection. He will come and I know Whisper holds one of the key to our case" Roni said confidently.

"Alright, let's go then!" Ian stood up from his chair, ready to face the challenges that lay ahead. But Roni held him back with a playful grin.

"You are gonna go like this?" Roni said.

"Why what is wrong? I got this dry-cleaned, we do not have much time. Let's just get this assh..." Ian said in a hurry.

"Hold on, boss. We can't just waltz into "The Haven" in our usual attire. We need to blend in and look important" Roni said teasingly.

"I knew there had to be a catch when you mentioned a party" Ian said smirking.

"Perks of being a detective, boss. You work while you party and you party while you work" Roni said laughing.

Ian followed Roni out of the office and they sat in Roni's Cadillac.

"Where are we heading?" Ian asked her.

"We are gonna get suit up and I know just the place" Roni said cutting a corner with little to no care. She stopped in front of a lavish boutique.

Ian and Roni entered a lavish boutique, filled with elegant dresses and sharp suits. Roni's eyes sparkled with excitement as she scanned the racks of clothes.

"How about this one, boss? It's sleek and sophisticated, perfect for the occasion" she said pointing at one dress.

"Roni, I think that dress costs more than my monthly salary" Ian said smirking teasingly.

"Well, boss, tonight we're not just any ordinary detective duo. We're going undercover among the criminal elite. We need to look the part and besides it's all going in the D.A's account. She says she will go to any lengths to catch our guy and wants us to do the same" Roni said holding up a credit card in her hand.

"Wow, you really are making the most of your post as a detective for the high and mighty Samantha Williams" Ian said running his finger on a row of sleek looking dinner jackets.

"Hey I worked hard for this!" Roni said furrowing her brow.

"I am not saying it is not well deserved ok? Alright! Let's do it. Find something that won't make me stick out like a sore thumb" Ian said giving up.

Roni's face lit up like the 4th of July and she eagerly picked out an impeccable tuxedo for Ian and a dazzling black gown for herself. They headed to the dressing rooms to change.

Inside the dressing rooms, Ian struggled with his bowtie while Roni adjusted her dress in the mirror.

"I've never been good at tying these things" Ian said grumbling.

"Don't worry, boss. I've got you covered. You focus on looking dashing, and I'll take care of the bowtie" Roni said chuckling from her changing room.

"Allow me", Ian got startled as Roni stepped behind him, expertly tying his bowtie with a flourish.

"There you go, boss. You're now the epitome of debonair" Roni said admiring her work.

"I must say, Roni, you've got a hidden talent for this. You could've been a fashion designer" Ian said, genuinely impressed.

"Well, being a detective keeps me on my toes, boss. I have to be a jack of all trades" Roni said with pride.

Once dressed, Ian and Roni made their way to the location in Nevada. As they approached the sprawling villa surrounded by mountains, they marveled at its grandeur.

Ian said whispering, "Roni, I hope our cover doesn't get blown. These criminals can be quite perceptive."

"I know chief and it is going to help us a lot if we do not use our real names" Roni said sarcastically.

"Right. Sorry, 'Willow' " Ian said with a fake smile.

"Trust me, boss. We've done this before. We'll blend in seamlessly" Roni said confidently.

They reached the entrance of the villa, where a line of elegantly dressed guests waited to enter. Roni showed their invitations to the doorman, who nodded and gestured for them to proceed.

"Welcome Mr. Wayne and Ms. Willow. This way" the doorman said handing two masks to them.

Inside, the grand hall was adorned with opulent decorations and dimly lit chandeliers. The sound of laughter and murmurs filled the air as guests mingled, their faces hidden behind intricately designed masks.

"This place is like something out of a movie" Ian said surveying the place. "Let's split and look for Whisper" Ian said.

"Agreed, boss. We'll rendezvous near the bar in an hour" Roni said nodding.

They parted ways, blending into the crowd, observing conversations and looking for any sign of their target. Ian discreetly eavesdropped on a group of well-dressed gentlemen discussing a recent heist.

"Quite the successful operation, I must say. That heist went off without a hitch" said a man with a squeaky voice.

"Indeed, my friend. We executed it flawlessly. The security never stood a chance" said one of them.

Ian's ears perked up at the mention of a heist. He leaned in closer, pretending to examine a painting on the nearby wall, while intently listening to their conversation.

"So, what was the prize this time? Jewels? Artifacts? Something more extravagant, perhaps?" said an elderly gentleman sipping his wine.

"Oh, you wouldn't believe it. It was the Crown Jewels themselves. We made off with a fortune" the guy with the squeaky voice said with pride.

Ian's eyes widened, astonished by the audacity of the theft. He knew he had stumbled upon a major lead but it did not concern him. He was there for Whisper.

"The authorities are clueless, my friends. We left no trace behind. It was a masterful display of skill and those idiots will never find out who did it" said one voice from behind a mask.

Ian mentally took note of the confident demeanor and the lack of remorse in their voices. These gentlemen were clearly experienced and dangerous criminals and his blood boiled at their confidence.

"Any plans for the next operation? I heard rumors of a rare diamond being showcased at the museum downtown" said the one with the squeaky voice.

"Ah, yes. That diamond has caught our attention too. But we'll bide our time. It's all about timing, my friend" said the deep voice.

Ian's mind raced as he absorbed the information, his detective instincts guiding him to the heart of the criminal underworld. As much as he wanted to see these guys talking about the heist behind bars he could not do anything.

Just as Ian was about to leave, one of them turned to him and asked "Excuse me Sir, have we met before?"

"May be, May be not. You know how it is here. Your voice sounds pretty familiar too" Ian said confidently.

"I was just wondering if you would like to share your thoughts on what we were discussing" said the elderly gentleman in a scrutinizing tone.

"I am sorry I do not like to listen to people's conversation without their consent. It is bad manners. I was just looking at this painting…" Just as Ian thought his cover was about to be blown, a voice cut through the air.

"Excuse me can I steal Mr. Wayne from you for a bit" Roni said putting her hand over Ian's shoulder.

Ian smiled through the mask and said "Excuse me gentleman I have to take this."

"Thank you Roni. They were discussing the jewel heist. I could not resist" Ian said with guilt.

"Focus. This place is swarming with criminals. If we arrest them all the prisons are going to over flow, besides they will catch us before we catch them. I do not want to be tied to a cactus in a dress you feelin' me?" Roni said as she skillfully maneuvered through the crowd.

"Boss, I overheard some interesting details about a secret meeting. I think Whisper might be involved. We need to find out more" Roni said whispering in Ian's ear. "I heard whispers about a hidden room in the basement. It's supposed to be where the real deals go down. That's our best bet" she added.

"All right, lead the way" Ian said.

Ian and Roni discreetly made their way towards the basement, ready to face the dangers that awaited them in "The Haven." When they reached the end of the maze it revealed a big room with people sitting in front of screens typing away.

"Wow, this place has more computers and technology than a tech expo" Ian said in an impressed tone.

"And more weapons than an arsenal" Roni said pointing to the grenade launchers that were set to be sold on a table elegantly.

"We are at the right place all right!" Ian said scanning the room.

As they cautiously made their way through the maze-like structure, a figure emerged from the darkness. It was Whisper, his face concealed by a mask and his voice disguised, an embodiment of secrecy.

"I believe you are looking for me" he said in his mysterious voice. He was wearing a mask adorned by jewels.

Ian's heart raced as he approached Whisper, his voice laced with anticipation. "We've been searching for you, Whisper. We believe you hold the key to uncovering the truth about Simon Grunfeld."

Whisper's eyes gleamed with a mix of curiosity and wariness. "Why should I trust you? What's in it for me? You could be cops."

"We can offer you protection, a chance to expose the darkness that has lingered for far too long. Together, we can get Simon out. He is the enemy of my enemy" Ian met his gaze, his voice steady.

Whisper remained silent for a moment, his masked face unreadable. Then, he nodded slowly. "Very well. I will share what I know. I do not need anything in return but you have to pay the ghost. Come with me." With that, Whisper led Ian and Roni deeper into The Haven.

As Ian followed Whisper through the dimly lit corridors, a palpable sense of anticipation filled the air. The whispers of conversations and muffled footsteps echoed around them, creating an eerie ambiance that seemed to mirror the weight of the secrets hidden within these walls.

Passing through a heavy metal door, they entered a room bathed in a soft, ethereal glow. The space was filled with an eclectic mix of individuals, their faces too obscured by masks or half-hidden in the shadows. Ian's senses sharpened as he surveyed the room, trying to discern who among them might hold the key to unlocking Simon's true identity.

Whisper led them to a secluded corner, away from prying eyes and ears. There, surrounded by an air of secrecy, he began to share fragments of his knowledge, each word laced with caution.

"I've encountered 'The Monkey' on several occasions," Whisper whispered, his voice barely audible above the hushed murmurs in the room. "He's a master of disguise, a chameleon who can seamlessly blend into any environment. He leaves no trace, no breadcrumb for you to follow."

Ian's brow furrowed, his mind racing to make sense of the puzzle. "But surely there must be something, someone who can provide us with more concrete information about him?"

Whisper's eyes flickered with a mix of melancholy and determination. "There is one name that has surfaced in whispers and half-truths. They call her 'The Oracle,' a woman rumored to possess a wealth of information, a keeper of secrets who can peer into the darkest recesses of the criminal underworld. I work for her and I know that she had the evidence you seek."

Roni leaned in, her voice filled with anticipation. "Do you know how we can find her? We need to reach her, to unravel the truth surrounding Simon."

Whisper hesitated for a moment, contemplating the risks involved. Then, with a resolute nod, he replied, "There is a hidden network, a secret society operating at Caesar's, accessible only to those with the right connections. It is there that you might find the Oracle, but be warned, gaining entry won't be easy."

Ian's determination surged within him, fueled by the prospect of uncovering the truth. "We will find a way. We must."

As Ian, Roni, and Whisper stood in the dimly lit corner of the lavish mansion, Whisper turned to Ian and Roni, a serious expression on his face.

"Ian, Roni, I want you to meet JR," Whisper said, gesturing toward a man standing nearby. "He'll be your guide as you venture into the secrets of the archive of Caesar. JR, these are my friends who were looking for me I mentioned earlier."

"Hey there!" JR said shaking their hands.

Ian's eyes widened in surprise as tried to remember the familiar voice. It was Jack Dill, the informer they were supposed to meet in Vegas.

"Hi Mr. Dil," Ian said in a blank tone masking his own voice.

A mix of shock and realization crossed Jack's face "You guys are good? How did you know it was me?"

"Small world" Whisper said laughing for the first time.

"I know him. We were to go look for him in Vegas" Ian turned to Whisper and said.

A wry smile played on Jack's lips as he nodded. "Yes. It seems we've been playing a game of cat and mouse without even realizing it. I was Whisper's eyes and years for a long time and I've been providing you with information too. Now that I know you are Whisper's friend and one of us. I will let you in on the big secret at the Caesars"

Roni chimed in, "So, you were Whisper's eyes and ears within the Caesar's too?"

Jack nodded again, confirming her assumption. "That's correct. I infiltrated the society years ago, gaining their trust and access to their gatherings. It was the only way I could keep track of their movements and potentially get valuable information. Information people will pay for."

"Jack has been a crucial asset in our fight against the law. He has taken great risks to stay undercover, and now he will guide you into the archive of Caesar, a place shrouded in mystery and danger" Whisper said.

Ian understood the gravity of the situation. Jack's role as their informer had been instrumental in their progress, and now, he would be their ally in navigating the treacherous waters of the hidden archive.

"Thank you, Jack," Ian said, gratitude evident in his voice. "Your assistance has been invaluable, and I'm honored to have you by our side as we enter the archive. With your help, we may finally get the answers we seek about Simon."

Jack's smile softened, and he nodded with sincerity. "I wish you both the best of luck. Now, if you'll excuse me, I must depart for urgent business. But I'm confident that you'll find what you're looking for in the archive. I will see you there. Will be there with more yet valuable information."

As Ian and Roni left the Haven, they were quite eager to get the required information from Jack. But they still had to wait for two days. Will Ian get more information about Simon? Or all of his questions will go unanswered.

During the two days of waiting, Ian's anticipation grew with each passing moment. He couldn't help but wonder if Jack would provide the crucial information they needed to finally unravel the mysteries surrounding Simon. The weight of unanswered questions pressed heavily upon him, fueling a mix of anxiety and determination.

Chapter 6

In the heart of the desert, where shimmering mirages dance beneath an eternal sun, lies a city draped in mystery. Las Vegas, a nocturnal oasis amidst the arid embrace, conceals secrets within its neon-lit streets and luxurious facades. It is a place where shadows merge with extravagant excess, where fortunes are won and lost, and where both big and small criminals find solace in the depths of their deceptions.

In this den of chance and opportunity, where the line between truth and falsehood blurs with each roll of the dice, those who bear the weight of their illicit deeds seek refuge. They arrive, cloaked in the guise of gamblers and thrill-seekers, adorned with the spoils of their unlawful endeavors. It is here that the city opens its arms, embracing the broken souls seeking sanctuary from the prying eyes of justice.

The grandiose casinos, palaces of chance and destiny, stand as towering sentinels that guard the secrets of the night. Within their opulent halls, masked identities melt into a sea of anonymity. The clatter of chips, the cacophony of spinning roulette wheels, and the hushed whispers of whispered conversations provided a symphony that masked the darker intentions lurking in the shadows.

High above the city, penthouses in gleaming towers serve as lairs for those who have woven intricate webs of deceit. Their ill-gotten gains are exchanged discreetly for chips, their tainted pasts concealed beneath the ripples of lavish excess. The city's sins are but whispers in the wind, lost amidst the ostentatious displays of wealth and indulgence.

But like the shifting sands of the desert that surround it, Las Vegas is not easily tamed. It is a place where fortune favors the bold and the cunning but where the price of arrogance can be steep. For amidst the glitz and glamour, the eyes of fate watch unblinkingly, waiting to unravel the intricate tapestry of deceit that has been woven.

The night swallowed the desolate highway as Detective Ian and Roni rode in Roni's black Cadillac toward the glittering abyss of Las Vegas once more. The silence between them hung heavy, punctuated only by the low hum of the engine. The vehicle glided smoothly down the highway, devouring the miles that separated them from their destination. The moon cast a pale glow upon the desert landscape, accentuating the solitude of their mission as Steely Dan played on the car radio.

"Now you swear and kick and beg us that you're not a gamblin' man...

Then you find you're back in Vegas with a handle in your hand...

Your black cards can make you money so you hide them when you're able...

In the land of milk and honey, you must put them on the table...

You go back, Jack, do it again, wheels turnin' 'round and 'round...

You go back, Jack, do it again..."

As the engine hummed in the background, Roni broke the silence, "I know you are going to be upset, Chief, but... you should have listened to me about Simon. I trust your hunch, but this time I knew he was a dead end from the start. We wasted precious time going back from halfway to talk to him instead of Jack that day."

Ian turned his gaze toward Roni, his eyes reflecting the weight of their shared pursuit. "Veronica, sometimes we have to chase those dead ends to clear the path ahead. I needed to talk to him before I talked to anyone else. Simon may not have given me what I wanted, but we needed to talk to him to move past him and explore other options like this informer the D.A. set up."

Roni sighed, her grip on the steering wheel tightening. "I get it, Ian. We have to explore every lead and turn over every stone. But the clock is ticking, and we are going nowhere with this case. I just hope that with the claims Whisper made, Jack delivers something concrete, or his ass is grass."

A flicker of determination danced in Ian's eyes as he leaned back, his voice filled with conviction. "And that's why we're heading to Vegas, Roni. We're going to meet JR Dill and dig deeper. Simon was just a stepping stone, a necessary detour to get us here."

Roni nodded a hint of admiration in her gaze. "I suppose you always have a method to your madness, eh? Well, let's hope Jack holds the information we've been searching for."

As they approached the dazzling lights of the Las Vegas Strip, the Cadillac's purr grew louder, resonating with anticipation. Roni expertly maneuvered through the bustling streets, guiding the car toward the grandeur of Caesar's Palace with pride. The valet attendant, a short young man with a wide grin, greeted them as they pulled up.

"Nice ride you got there," the valet commented, eyeing the sleek Cadillac appreciatively.

Roni nodded, a smirk playing at the corner of her lips. "Thanks, kid. Just make sure you treat her well and don't scratch a thing."

She tossed the key toward the valet, who caught it deftly. "No worries, ma'am. She'll be in good hands."

With a final nod of approval, Detective Ian and Roni strode into the opulent halls of Caesar's Palace. The air buzzed with the intoxicating energy of the city, a symphony of clinking glasses and hushed conversations weaving together.

As they found a discreet corner to wait, Roni's gaze wandered, her eyes seeing beautiful women that traversed the casino floor. A mischievous smile played on her lips as she leaned toward Ian.

"Some quality time to spend with these hotties of Las Vegas like a normal person? It's a city that knows how to make a man forget his worries, stay longer, and you will forget your wife and kids."

Ian chuckled softly, shaking his head. "I am more focused on having the criminal spend time behind bars. We're here for a reason, remember?"

"Let's not forget that!" Ian said with a smile.

Roni nodded, smiling mischievously, her attention returning to the task at hand. "Of course, Ian. Just making sure you don't lose the finer things in life while we're chasing monkeys."

Time slipped away in the vibrant chaos of the casino, each passing minute reminding them of the urgency of their mission. And then, like a whisper in the crowd, Detective Ian's eyes caught a glimpse of JR discreetly scanning the room. He nudged Roni, drawing her attention to him.

"Looks like our guy is here," Ian whispered, his voice edged with anticipation. "Let's go."

As they approached him with measured and purposeful steps, it was the first time they were seeing him without a mast. They noticed that day that Jack's rugged face bore the marks of a life lived on the edge, his weathered complexion telling tales of long nights and countless secrets. His dark eyes were sharp and observant, which held a glimmer of hidden knowledge, a testament to the risks he had taken and the choices he had made.

A slight graying peppered his unkempt hair, adding to the air of experience that surrounded him. Jack's lean frame exuded a quiet confidence, hinting at the resilience that had sustained him through the shadows he navigated.

Dressed in a suit, the fabric subtly frayed in places, Jack blended effortlessly into the background of the bustling casino. His attire mirrored the subtle balance he maintained between the worlds of law enforcement and the criminal underbelly, never fully committing to one side.

As Detective Ian and Roni stood in front of him, Jack's eyes met theirs, recognizing the shared purpose that brought them together. His gaze held a mix of caution and resolved, a sign of the risks he had taken to gather the information that awaited them.

"Detective Ian, Detective Roni," Jack greeted them with a nod, his voice a low rasp. "Glad you could make it."

Ian's expression remained guarded yet hopeful. "Sure, let's find somewhere more private to talk, Jack. Lead the way."

Jack guided them through the labyrinth of the casino, skillfully navigating the maze of flashing lights and clattering slot machines. They reached a secluded corner, shielded from prying eyes and ears.

Once seated, Ian leaned forward, his eyes fixed on Jack. "So, what do you have for us, Jack? We've been chasing shadows for too long."

Jack leaned back, a knowing smile playing on his lips. "I've got the missing piece of the puzzle you've been searching for. The key to unlocking the truth lies within the hidden archive of Caesar."

Roni's interest piqued, and her gaze fixed on Jack. "What can you tell us about it?"

Jack's eyes scanned their surroundings, ensuring their conversation remained shielded from prying ears. The room was secure, devoid of any surveillance devices that could compromise their mission. Satisfied with their privacy, Jack leaned in closer, his voice dropping to a low, conspiratorial whisper.

"The archive of Caesar is the best-kept secret in Vegas's history. They are the administration that runs all things illegal in the desert. They're the unseen puppeteers, pulling strings in the shadows of this city. Drug trafficking, money laundering, extortion—you name it, they're involved. Their grip on Las Vegas is tighter than anyone realizes, and anyone who had operated in Vegas respects them for they value talent and courage."

Ian's expression hardened, a spark of determination igniting within him. "You are saying that this syndicate knows about the person we are looking for?"

Jack leaned in closer; his voice lowered to a near-whisper. "Exactly, I've been in contact with them for years.

I have been gathering evidence on people you want. Robbers, frauds, murderers, rapists, and drug dealers so that I can get a clean slate in return. I can provide you with enough proof to apprehend your guy. But it will come with a cost. No freebies in Vegas."

Roni's eyes widened, a mix of excitement and caution emanating from her. "Are you sure you're willing to take that risk, Jack? Exposing yourself could be dangerous."

Jack's face hardened, lines etched deeper by the weight of his memories. "I've made my choice. I need to start new, no matter the cost. And with your reputation, I believe I can trust you guys. I am helping you so you can help me get the fuck out of here with a new identity."

Ian nodded his voice firm. "We won't let your sacrifice be in vain, Jack. We'll protect you."

"As much as I trust you, I do not want to end up dead. Before I hand myself over to you, I want my new identity written in black and white. I want myself a freeman in the eyes of the law before I spill the tea," Jack said low-key, pleading to them.

He took a deep breath and continued, "I have done horrible things to get you the evidence you want. Do not let it go in vain, Detectives. I cannot disclose any information right now. I will leave now; my associate will find you in the Casino and brief you on the evidence. I will be in contact" Jack rose from his seat and darted out of the main door.

Detective Ian and Roni rose from their seats, ready to face what awaited them. Jack Dill, their unexpected ally, had become their beacon of hope in this puzzle of a case. As they left the secluded corner, stepping back into the pulsating heart of Caesar's Palace, Ian's gaze met Roni's. A shared understanding passed between them.

They made their way back to the casino floor, their expressions resolute. The air seemed to crackle with renewed energy as they navigated through the maze of flashing lights and eager gamblers. The charm of the city's vices now faded into the background as a more pressing mission beckoned them forward.

Their eyes scanned the crowd, searching for any signs of Jack's associate. The glitz and glamour of the casino masked the insidious workings of the criminal empire, but their gut feeling told them that they were being watched closely.

Suddenly, a tap on Detective Ian's shoulder sent a shiver of anticipation down his spine. He turned to find himself face-to-face with a woman who exuded an aura of both magic and mystery. Her presence was captivating, drawing his gaze to her with an almost magnetic pull.

Her lustrous, midnight-black hair cascaded in waves, framing a face that could launch a thousand ships. Her almond-shaped eyes, a mesmerizing shade of emerald green, held a hint of mischief. They seemed to hold secrets untold, and Ian and Roni found themselves instantly intrigued.

"Welcome, Mr. Ian and Ms. Roni. I believe that you are friends of Mr. Jack," she asked, her voice barely above a whisper.

"Well… he is not our… 'friend' per se, but we are his safest option if he wants to get out of the mess he has landed himself into alive and without holes," Roni said, eyeing the woman.

"Ian, it's a pleasure to meet you" Ian introduced himself and took her hand in his before planting a kiss on the back.

"A man of culture," she said, smiling. "I am the Oracle. Please follow me, but we need to move quickly. There are eyes everywhere."

Ian and Roni exchanged a glance, instinctively recognizing a potential ally in their midst. Without a word, they followed her.

"Easy there, Caligula," said Roni to Ian in a whisper as they followed Oracle through a hidden passage concealed behind a curtain of cascading water. The murmurs of the casino faded into the distance as they entered a dimly lit corridor, its walls adorned with framed photographs of past glory.

Ian was not surprised by how Roni was acting around her. She was the epitome of beauty and mystique. High cheekbones added a touch of regality to her features, while her perfectly arched brows hinted at a keen intellect that lay beneath her captivating exterior. A delicate nose and softly curved, rosy-hued lips completed her alluring visage, leaving Ian unable to tear his eyes away.

Her slender, graceful figure was accentuated by a form-fitting black dress that clung to her every curve, hinting at the allure that lay beneath the fabric. The dress dipped enticingly at the neckline, leaving just enough to the imagination, while a thigh-high slit teased a glimpse of smooth, sun-kissed skin.

Every movement she made was graceful, a subtle sway of her hips that seemed to command attention without uttering a word. Her posture was poised, hinting at a hidden strength that belied her feminine allure.

"This is the archive of Caesar, or The Underground as you say," Oracle explained, her voice filled with a hint of urgency. "A secret network of informers and moderators running the show in Vegas. We operate in the shadows, preventing the hell from bleeding in this heaven and providing refuge and a safe haven to the tormented souls."

Roni's eyes widened, her curiosity piqued. "How did you find us? How do you know what we are searching for?"

Oracle smiled wickedly. "We have eyes everywhere, Detective. We've been monitoring your investigation, waiting for the right moment to make contact. Jack has been valuable to us. He has done the archive's bidding, and now we are fulfilling our promise by giving you what you need under the agreement that JR will live as a freeman."

Ian's gaze hardened, determination etched across his features. "You have our word. We can't afford to waste any more time. Show us what you have."

As they delved deeper into the archives, Oracle revealed a hidden chamber filled with meticulously organized files, surveillance footage, and intricate webs of interconnected information. The room was filled with evidence of malpractice and crime that could put Mafias and billionaires out of business for good.

The air was thick with anticipation as they approached a large screen mounted on the wall. Oracle swiftly moved to a control panel, her fingers dancing across the buttons and switches with practiced ease. The screen flickered to life, revealing a surveillance video from a museum. The footage showed the quiet stillness of a grand exhibition hall, the paintings and artifacts bathed in a soft glow.

Suddenly, the silence was shattered as a figure emerged from the shadows, appearing seemingly out of thin air. Dressed in sleek black, its body clad in skin-tight clothes, the mysterious intruder moved with a fluid grace that defied human limitations. It was as if they possessed a feral agility akin to that of a nimble monkey navigating its surroundings.

Ian and Roni's eyes widened with astonishment as they watched the criminal scale the walls of the museum, effortlessly climbing like a creature born for such feats. Their movements were a mesmerizing dance, each calculated step bringing them closer to their objective.

With astonishing precision, the intruder dismantled the cameras that dotted the ceiling, leaping from one chandelier to another, a balletic display of athleticism. Their actions were swift and deliberate, leaving no trace of their presence behind.

As the figure drew nearer to the camera that recorded the surveillance footage, Oracle paused the video, freezing the frame right when the culprit was facing the camera. The image displayed on the screen revealed a face hidden beneath a mask.

Ian's heart skipped a beat as he stared at the frozen image, his mind struggling to process what he was seeing. But deep down, a sense of recognition stirred within him. He couldn't deny what his eyes were revealing to him, he had seen those eyes before.

"It can't be," Ian whispered, his voice filled with a mixture of shock and disbelief. "That's... Simon," he whispered to himself.

Roni's expression mirrored Ian's astonishment, her eyes fixed on the frozen frame that captured the face of their former suspect. The revelation sent shockwaves through their investigation, opening up a whole new realm of questions and possibilities.

Oracle's eyes flickered with concern as she watched their reactions. She understood the weight of the revelation and the implications it carried for their mission.

"Ian," Oracle spoke softly, her voice laced with urgency. "You have to be careful. Simon's involvement with the LAPD runs deeper than you realize. He's dangerous, and he's been playing a game of shadows for a long time."

Ian's gaze hardened, his focus rekindled by the revelation. "We'll give Jack what he wants, expose the truth, and bring Simon to justice. We owe it to the people who have suffered because of his crimes."

Roni nodded in agreement, a steely resolve replacing her initial shock. "We'll stay connected with you, Oracle. Thank you for your help."

"Stay vigilant, detectives. We'll be watching, ready to lend our support as long as you reciprocate," Oracle said, looking into Ian's eyes.

With their mission reignited and the truth of Simon's involvement exposed, Detective Ian and Roni bid Oracle farewell, their steps resolute as they left the hidden chamber behind. Caesar's Palace faded into the distance as they drove out into the neon-lit streets of Las Vegas once again, ready to confront Simon.

Detective Ian seethed with a mixture of anger and frustration as he replayed the surveillance footage of Simon's criminal exploits in his head. The realization that he had been deceived gnawed at him, fueling a fiery determination to uncover the truth hidden behind Simon's mask of innocence.

His fists clenched involuntarily as he remembered the footage, each movement of Simon's calculated and deliberate. The weight of betrayal settled heavily on Ian's shoulders, his mind replaying their last meeting.

Roni sensed Ian's seething anger and approached him cautiously, her voice laced with concern. "What do we do now?"

Ian turned to face her, his eyes burning with a fierce resolve. "We confront him, Roni. We go back to him, and this time, we won't hold back. I'll extract the truth from him by any means necessary."

Roni studied Ian's determined expression, recognizing the fire that burned within her partner. She knew Ian's pursuit of justice was relentless, and at that moment, nothing could deter him from seeking the truth.

"All right then," Roni replied, her tone steady. "But we have to be careful. Simon is clever, and he won't give up his secrets easily."

Ian nodded, his mind already spinning with strategies and scenarios. "We'll gather all the evidence we have against him, every piece that connects him to the murders. We'll corner him and solve this mystery once and for all."

In the depths of his heart, Ian vowed that this time there would be no room for doubt. He would leave no stone unturned, sparing no effort in extracting the truth from Simon's elusive facade. The betrayal would not be forgotten, and justice would prevail.

As they neared their destination, Ian's fury burned brighter, fanning the flames of his determination. Simon may have deceived him once, but this time, he would not escape the consequences of his actions. Ian was ready to confront him, to face the storm head-on and unearth the secrets that lay buried beneath Simon's facade of innocence. The time for games was over. The truth would be revealed, no matter the cost. It was time to confront the monkey.

Chapter 7

The sound of the engine faded into the night as the sleek black Jaguar came to a halt in the D.A.'s driveway. The figure that emerged from the car was cloaked in darkness, their face hidden beneath the shadow of a hood. With a purposeful stride, they slung a bag over their shoulder and made their way towards the backyard.

The night seemed to hold its breath, anticipating the impending intrusion. The figure moved with practiced grace, their steps soundless as they approached the back door. With a skill born of familiarity, they manipulated the lock, allowing themselves silent passage into the house.

As the figure ventured further into the dimly lit house, its senses heightened. Each creak of the floorboard sent a chill down their spine. But they pressed on, driven by an unknown objective. The stairs beckoned, promising secrets waiting to be unveiled.

Just as the figure reached the bottom step, their heart pounding in their chest, the darkness was shattered by the sudden illumination of lights. In the lounge, sitting upon a large chair, was William Katz, his smoky eyes fixed upon the intruder.

A sly smile played at the corner of William's lips as he took a leisurely puff of his Cuban cigar. "Why are you sneaking into your own house like a criminal, Samantha? You are the D.A., remember?" he said, his voice dripping with sarcasm.

Samantha, the mysterious figure, froze in her tracks, caught off guard by William's unexpected presence. Her hand instinctively went to her chest, her breath shallow. "You scared me, honey! I didn't want to wake you up, so I was being extra cautious not to make any noise," she replied, her voice laced with feigned sweetness.

A chuckle escaped William's lips, the smoke from his cigar curling around him like a wisp of suspicion. "Honey, you could have woken me up if you were going somewhere. It's 3 a.m. in the morning. Where did you go that late? You didn't have to wait for me to sleep to leave, you know," he retorted, his tone dripping with sarcasm.

Samantha moved closer to William, her eyes locking onto his, searching for a hint of vulnerability. She delicately perched herself on his lap, her voice laced with a hint of playfulness. "Oh, no, dear. It's not like that. After you fell asleep, I went to the study to review a file. I realized I left it at my desk in the office, so I went to get it," she explained, her words seemingly innocent.

The lines on William's forehead deepened, his gaze piercing as he stared into Samantha's eyes. "You've been working late at night a lot these days. It's the third time you've snuck out. What's the meaning of this?" he questioned, his voice tinged with suspicion.

Samantha held his gaze, her expression unwavering, as she presented the file she had retrieved. "Snuck out? No, honey, it's not like that. You know you can trust me. Look, I got this file, and see the date on it," she said, her voice steady as she offered him evidence of her supposed innocence.

William scrutinized the file, his brows furrowing as he weighed Samantha's words against his lingering doubts. "That's all fine and dandy, but you could have come through the front door. It's your own house. Why did you have to climb the fence like a monkey and come through the back door?" he interrogated, his eyes narrowing in suspicion.

Samantha let out a light laugh, her arms winding around William's neck, her touch attempting to dissipate his growing unease. "Oh, yes, about that, silly me. I forgot the keys, so I had to use the backdoor. I'm sorry if I startled you, honey," she explained, her voice dripping with contrition.

William chuckled, the tension in the room momentarily broken. "Startled me? Your face looks like you've just seen a ghost," he said, a genuine smile now gracing his lips.

Samantha, ever the master of composure, joined in his laughter, skillfully deflecting his suspicions. "You're just getting worried over nothing, Will. Let me make us some coffee, and then we can go back to sleep," she suggested, her words carrying a hint of reassurance.

William looked at her with questioning eyes, his doubts momentarily assuaged. He shook off the suspicion that had clouded his mind, deciding to trust his wife. "Sure, hon. I would love that," he replied, as Samantha rose from his lap and made her way toward the kitchen.

The aroma of freshly brewed coffee filled the kitchen, enveloping the space in a comforting embrace. Samantha's hands rested on the cool countertop as she watched the minutes tick away on the clock. Her gaze was distant, lost in deep thought as she mulled over her next course of action.

Unbeknownst to William, Samantha had been feeling the weight of his growing suspicion, and it gnawed at her. She couldn't afford to have him digging deeper, uncovering the truth behind her late-night activities. A plan formed in her mind, a desperate attempt to keep him at bay.

Muttering to herself, Samantha's voice carried a tinge of frustration. "I gotta do something about him or things will get out of hand. Imagine being caught by this dummy after everything," she whispered, her words filled with a mix of determination and exasperation.

The coffee finished brewing, its rich aroma infusing the air and adding warmth to the chilly night. Samantha turned her attention to the top shelf, her eyes scanning the array of items until she found what she was looking for—an innocuous-looking capsule. A wicked smile played at the corner of her lips.

"This ought to do it," she muttered under her breath, a sense of mischief gleaming in her eyes. She deftly opened the capsule and poured its contents into William's mug, the liquid blending seamlessly with the dark coffee. "This will shut him up good. I wonder why he didn't fall asleep before," she mused, her thoughts veering into the realm of deception.

Samantha stirred the coffee, her spoon swirling the murky liquid as the contents of the capsule dissolved, vanishing without a trace. It wasn't the first time she had resorted to such measures. William's growing skepticism had pushed her to take drastic measures, to ensure her own peace and freedom to work undisturbed.

With the coffee prepared, Samantha glanced over her shoulder, ensuring that William was nowhere in sight. Satisfied, she carefully reached for the cups, balancing them in her hands. Her footsteps were light and cautious as she made her way to their bedroom, where William lay on the bed, his gaze fixed on some distant point.

Setting the coffee on the nightstand, Samantha leaned over, her lips meeting his in a tender kiss. "I love you, baby. You don't have to worry about me going behind your back, cheating on you. You are my one and only," she whispered, her voice filled with false sincerity.

William took a sip of the coffee, his eyes never leaving the cup. "I'm not worried about cheating, Samantha. I'm worried about our safety, yours and mine," he stated matter-of-factly, his suspicion lingering beneath his words.

Samantha settled beside him on the bed, her eyes searching his face for any sign of doubt. "Don't worry, dear. We will be just fine," she reassured him, her voice a mere whisper, her heart pounding with a mix of guilt and desperation.

As the night wore on, the effects of the capsule began to take hold. William's eyes grew heavy, his body succumbing to the drowsiness that seeped through his veins. Samantha watched him, her emotions a jumble of relief and remorse. She shad bought herself some time, but at what cost?

The room fell into a hushed silence, broken only by the sound of William's soft snores. Samantha stared at his slumbering form, wrestling with her conscience. She had crossed a line, drugging her own husband, all in the name of self-preservation.

As darkness enveloped the room, Samantha was left alone with her thoughts. The thrilling and dangerous path she had chosen lay before her, the consequences of her actions looming like shadows in the night.

In the glamorous city of Los Angeles, where dreams were born and shattered under the weight of ambition, William Katz and Samantha Grundfeld's paths converged at a glittering fundraiser. Samantha, an ambitious and driven assistant district attorney, attended the event with her mentor and boss, Kirk Mullen, who held the esteemed position of D.A. at the time. William, on the other hand, was a charismatic and influential businessman, the epitome of success and the most sought-after bachelor in town.

As fate would have it, William and Samantha's eyes met across the crowded room, and an instant connection sparked between them. Their conversation flowed effortlessly, their laughter resonating through the air, as they discovered kindred spirits in one another. Their connection was undeniable, and they soon found themselves entangled in a whirlwind romance.

In a series of whirlwind events, their love deepened, and before long, they were engaged to be married. However, tragedy struck when Kirk Mullen met his untimely demise, falling from the roof of his penthouse under mysterious circumstances. Samantha, with her unwavering determination and drive, rose from the ashes and emerged as the newly elected district attorney.

With Samantha as the D.A. and William by her side, their union solidified into a power couple that commanded both respect and fear. Samantha's position allowed her to wield influence within the law enforcement department, while William's wealth and connections paved the way for their rapid ascent. Together, they pushed the boundaries of the legal and corporate world, their hunger for success surpassing all limits.

Yet, beneath the facade of their seemingly perfect partnership, a seed of doubt began to take root in William's mind. He sensed deceit lurking within the shadows, a whisper of deception that danced at the edge of his consciousness. His sharp intuition, honed through years of business acumen, warned him that something was amiss.

William's suspicions grew, like a festering wound that refused to heal. He confronted Samantha multiple times, questioning her actions, but each time she skillfully evaded his inquiries, weaving tales of innocence and dismissing his concerns as mere paranoia. She played her part flawlessly, convincing him that his doubts were unfounded.

However, William's astute nature refused to be silenced. He knew that his business ventures demanded his attention, and Samantha took advantage of this, using his preoccupation to cloak her own activities. The weight of responsibility and the demands of his empire left him little time to keep a watchful eye on his wife, but the nagging feeling in his gut persisted.

In the late hours of the night, when the city slumbered, William would find himself pondering over his thoughts and events for any shred of evidence that would validate his suspicions. The lines between his business acumen and his personal life blurred as he delved deeper into the labyrinth of deceit.

William discovered irregularities in Samantha's behavior, and mysterious connections that raised red flags. He knew he was onto something, but the full extent of Samantha's actions remained shrouded in darkness.

Haunted by uncertainty and plagued by the weight of his discoveries, William resolved to confront Samantha once and for all. He would demand the truth, regardless of the consequences. With a steely resolve, he prepared himself for the battle that lay ahead.

The stage was set. William awaited Samantha's return from a late-night meeting, his heart pounding with a mix of trepidation and determination. As the clock ticked closer to midnight, the sound of the front door opening shattered the stillness of the night.

Samantha entered, her features a mask of composure. Her eyes met William's, and for a fleeting moment, the flicker of unease passed across her face. But she quickly regained her poise, a smile playing at the corners of her lips. She moved toward him, her steps deliberate yet graceful.

"William, darling," she greeted him, her voice dripping with warmth and affection. "I didn't expect you to be awake at this hour."

William fixed her with a piercing gaze, his voice laced with a mix of suspicion and urgency. "Samantha, we need to talk. It's time to address the elephant in the room."

A flash of alarm flickered in Samantha's eyes, but she quickly masked it with a controlled smile. "Darling, whatever do you mean? We've been through this before. You're overthinking things, letting your imagination run wild."

William's voice hardened, his eyes never leaving Samantha's. "No more deflections, Samantha. I know something is going on, and I demand the truth."

Samantha's facade began to crack, her confidence wavering as she realized that her carefully constructed web of deceit was unraveling. She tried to regain her composure, to manipulate the situation as she had done before, but William's unwavering gaze pierced through her defenses.

With a heavy sigh, Samantha's demeanor shifted, her voice tinged with resignation. "You're right, William. I can no longer hide the truth from you. But know that I love you."

William nodded and Samantha walked up to him. Standing before William, she presented a small box from the pocket of her coat. Her eyes bore into his, a mixture of anticipation twinkling within them. William's brows furrowed, his curiosity piqued by the mysterious package. "What is this?" he inquired, his voice laced with a hint of caution.

A mischievous smile tugged at Samantha's lips as she issued a command, her tone leaving no room for hesitation. "Open it," she ordered, her voice carrying an air of authority.

William took the box from her, his gaze shifting between the package and Samantha's gaze. A flicker of uncertainty danced across his face, but he complied, his fingers gently prying open the lid. He looked up at Samantha one last time, searching for any hint or clue as to what lay within.

Samantha nodded in approval, her eyes glittering with a mix of excitement and satisfaction. As William lifted the lid, his frown curved into a smile, and his eyes widened with astonishment. "Surprise!" Samantha exclaimed, unable to contain her delight. "I got this for you. I left it in the office and went to great lengths to acquire it. It came all the way from Switzerland and there are only three of these in the world."

Within the box lay an exquisite wristwatch, its design intricate and elegant. Diamonds adorned its frame, sparkling with a brilliance that captivated William's gaze. His breath caught in his throat as he realized the significance of the gift. It was a masterpiece, one of only three in existence.

A sense of awe washed over him, washing away his suspicions, at least momentarily. "Samantha, this is... incredible. This is worth thousands of dollars!," he stammered, his voice filled with wonder. "I can't believe you went through all this trouble. It's truly remarkable."

Samantha's smile widened, her eyes gleaming with satisfaction. She had successfully diverted his attention, skillfully capturing his heart in the process. She had become an expert at evading his accusations, weaving excuses and explanations that left him doubting his own sanity.

For a brief moment, William forgot the doubts that had plagued him. He was enveloped in the warmth of Samantha's presence, her thoughtfulness sweeping away any trace of suspicion. His heart ached with guilt for ever doubting her intentions.

This intricate dance had become all too familiar to them. William had confronted Samantha numerous times, each time met with a convincing response, a well-crafted excuse that allowed her to slip away unscathed. She played her part flawlessly, eroding his confidence and making him question his own judgment.

In that moment, holding the precious gift she had bestowed upon him, William's doubts were momentarily silenced. Samantha's clever antics had taken their toll, and he began to question whether he was truly losing touch with reality.

Samantha watched him, her gaze filled with a mix of relief and triumph. She had once again succeeded in deflecting his suspicions, solidifying her position of power and control. She knew that as long as she held the upper hand, she could continue her clandestine activities, shrouded in the guise of innocence and love.

As the weight of guilt pressed upon him, William couldn't help but feel a pang of self-doubt. Had he allowed his own paranoia to cloud his judgment? Was he truly losing himself in a web of suspicion? Samantha's actions had effectively gaslighted him, making him second-guess his own sanity.

Yet, a sliver of doubt remained, a tiny ember of mistrust that continued to smolder within him. He knew deep down that he couldn't ignore the whispers of his intuition forever. The battle between his heart and his mind raged on, leaving him trapped in a web of uncertainty, where every word and action held a hidden motive.

As the moon cast an ethereal glow upon the sleeping city, Samantha woke up and checked on William. William's snores echoed in the room. Samantha made sure that he was sleeping soundly and then she got up from her bed and went out of her bedroom.

Silently, she slipped out of their bedroom, her feet barely making a sound as they touched the floor. Her mind was focused, her determination unyielding. She knew she had to act swiftly and without hesitation.

She moved through the house with the grace of a phantom. William lay in deep slumber, blissfully unaware of the events unfolding around him. A smile played at the corners of Samantha's lips as she came down the stairs.

Reaching the front door, Samantha stepped into the cool night air, the darkness embracing her like an old friend. Her car, a sleek and inconspicuous vehicle, awaited her in the driveway. The trunk, a secret compartment of her clandestine operations, held the key to her nocturnal activities.

With a deft movement, Samantha popped open the trunk, revealing a large sack nestled within. The weight of her secret cargo shifted beneath the confines of the bag.

The night seemed to hold its breath as Samantha retrieved the sack, her heart pounding in her chest. She glanced back at the house, ensuring that William remained fast asleep, undisturbed by her midnight rendezvous.

Returning to the house, Samantha moved with a purpose, her steps calculated and swift. She ascended the stairs, her mind focused on a hidden room, one that had been transformed into her private sanctuary.

In the guest room, she carefully shifted the bed to the side, revealing a corner of the room that concealed her clandestine activities. The carpet, once a barrier to her secrets, was lifted with practiced ease, exposing a loose tile beneath.

A glimmer of anticipation danced in Samantha's eyes as she removed the tile, revealing a wooden cellar hidden beneath the surface. The air grew heavy with a mixture of trepidation and excitement as she opened the cellar door, revealing the depths of her secret lair.

With a swift motion, she upended the sack, and a cascade of treasures rained down into the hidden chamber. Diamond watches tumbled through the air, glinting in the dim light, as they found their place amidst diamonds, watches, and bundles of cash, acquired through years of careful planning and cunning manipulation. Precious jewelry adorned with shimmering gemstones and bundles of cash lay in organized chaos, evidence of Samantha's success as a mastermind of illicit activities.

There was a reason behind it all, a purpose that drove Samantha to orchestrate these midnight rituals. She reveled in her secret identity, for she was not simply Samantha Williams, the devoted wife and esteemed district attorney. No, she was Samantha Grunfeld, a name erased from the records.

Her nights spent lulling William into a deep sleep with sedatives were not merely for his comfort but to ensure her freedom to execute her plans without his interference. With each passing night, she had slowly cultivated her empire, one that thrived in the shadows, hidden beneath the façade of their seemingly perfect life.

As Samantha closed the cellar door, her eyes gleamed with a mix of satisfaction and anticipation. The riches that lay beneath the surface fueled her ambitions, driving her to reach new heights of power and influence. William's trust and obliviousness had become her greatest assets, allowing her to manipulate their lives to her advantage.

The night resumed its silent vigil as Samantha retreated from her hidden sanctuary, the door closing behind her with a soft click. She moved back through the house, retracing her steps, her every movement calculated to avoid detection.

Returning to the bedroom, Samantha slipped beneath the covers, her heart pounding with exhilaration. As she closed her eyes, a knowing smile graced her lips. The world may see her as Samantha Williams, the dutiful wife and esteemed D.A., but deep down, she reveled in the thrill of being the mastermind orchestrating her own brand of chaos.

And so, she drifted off into a restless sleep, her mind ablaze with the possibilities that lay ahead, her dreams filled with the sparkle of diamonds and the intoxicating scent of power.

Chapter 8

Simon fell down sideways along with the chair he was tied to and his jaw against the floor made an awful sound. The sound you hear in your head when your jaw cracks, except that everyone heard it. Simon let out a loud howl of pain. "Leave me alone PIGS! You have me here for life. Fuckin' leave me alone."

Ian had never practiced that style of interrogation before and but he was at his wit's end. As soon as he saw Simon he banged his head on the table in his cellar and started beating him to a pulp. Ian had some unresolved issues with being made a fool of.

He saw clearly in the surveillance video evidence at the archives that Simon was the man who orchestrated those robberies 20 years back. This only meant that he was lying about being connected to these robberies and his accomplice is still at large running rampant leaving bodies behind.

Ian had offered him his utmost support and he lied in front of his face like the professional he was. When he was dealt with force he had gotten too hard from the harsh treatment at the L.A. county jail and did not break.

"Break! You piece of shit," said Ian kicking him in his gut.

"Whoa, easy there Chief" Roni stepped forward in between Ian and Simon.

Ian took a step back and looked at Roni who was shocked to see him acting like that. The C.O. had a satisfied look on his face, almost as if he was proud of the treatment Ian was giving Simon time to compose.

"What's wrong? Tired already? Why don't you take a donut break?" said Simon smiling through a bleeding mouth still lying on the floor.

Simon's words sent Ian back into a fit of rage. He quickly walked toward him and made him sit straight again.

"I am going to ask you once again Simon and if you do not tell me the name of your accomplice who is still running around L.A. leaving bodies behind, I will not go easy on you," Ian said.

"Try me!" Simon said with a blank face and received a devastating punch on his jaw by the Robert, which left him unconscious.

"Hey! HEY!" Ian said pushing him back.

"He'll be fine. Trust me, he's taken worse. That brute has hardened into one stubborn inmate. We need to break him somehow, get him to talk" Robert said defensively.

Roni looked concerned, but Ian's frustration intensified.

"We've tried everything! He won't give us anything!" Ian said rubbing his temple.

"Then there's only one option left, Ian. The shock room. It's extreme, but it's our last resort if we want any chance of extracting the truth from him" said Robert grimly.

Ian's face contorted with a mix of anger and resignation.

"Fine. We'll do it your way. But if anything goes wrong, it's on you" Ian said gritting his teeth.

They exit the cell, the heavy metal door slamming shut behind them, leaving Simon unconscious on the chair.

Ian, Roni, and Robert walked briskly down the dimly lit corridor, their conversation hushed but intense.

"This is a dangerous path we're treading on Robert. The shock room is inhumane," said Ian still frustrated.

Robert (Sympathetic)

"I know it's not ideal, Ian. But desperate times call for desperate measures. If we want to bring down the people responsible for these murders, we need to extract information by any means necessary," said Robert sympathetically.

Roni's gaze shifts between Ian and Robert concern etched on her face. "I hope it doesn't come to that, but if it's our only option" Roni stopped in the middle of the sentence to judge the expressions on both men's faces.

Ian sighed heavily, his frustration mingled with a sense of duty.

"We have to do what it takes. Let's hope it doesn't break him completely," Ian said.

The full moon in the sky illuminated the prison yard as Ian, Roni, and the Robert stepped outside, the weight of their impending decision-hanging heavy in the air. They found a secluded spot near the perimeter fence, away from prying eyes and curious ears.

Ian paced back and forth, his frustration now mixed with a sense of guilt. "I can't believe it's come to this. We're resorting to torture to get information," Ian said with his voice filled with guilt.

Roni placed a comforting hand on Ian's shoulder, her voice gentle "We've exhausted every other option, Ian. We're running out of time, and lives are at stake. We have to do what we can to protect the innocent."

Robert against the fence, his gaze fixed on the distant horizon. "I understand your concerns, Ian. No one wants it to come to this. But sometimes, the line between justice and morality gets blurred. Our duty is to protect and serve, even when faced with difficult choices."

Ian stopped pacing and looked directly at Robert his eyes filled with determination, "I won't deny that we have to find those responsible, but we need to make sure that Simon's rights are not completely disregarded. We must minimize the harm inflicted on him."

Robert nodded in agreement, his expression serious. "Rest assured, Ian, we'll take every precaution necessary. We'll ensure he's not pushed beyond his limits, and we'll closely monitor the process," he said assuring.

Roni, her voice tinged with concern, spoke up. "What if this doesn't work? What if Simon still refuses to talk, even after the shock room?" she said hesitantly.

Ian's eyes harden, his frustration now focused into a steely resolve. "Then, Roni, we'll find another way. We won't give up until we uncover the truth. But we have to exhaust every option available to us."

The three of them stood there for a moment, contemplating the weight of their decision. The distant sound of a prison bell echoed through the yard, signalling the end of their conversation.

"Let's get back inside. We'll proceed cautiously, step by step. You will call the shots I will just facilitate and help you to the best of my abilities," Robert said supportively.

Ian nodded, his determination unwavering. "We'll do what needs to be done, but we'll do it right. No matter the outcome, we'll ensure justice is served," he said confidently.

They took a final moment to gather themselves before heading back into the prison, ready to face the harrowing task that lay ahead.

After walking the long corridor, Ian, Roni, and Robert stood before a heavy, reinforced door, the entrance to the dreaded shock room. The corridor leading to it was dimly lit, the atmosphere heavy with anticipation. Roni turned to Robert her brow furrowed with concern.

"Robert, why aren't the guards taking Simon to the shock room? Shouldn't he be here by now?" she asked curiously.

"The guards are way ahead of us, Roni. They've already taken Simon inside and made the necessary preparations. We just need to join them" Robert said confidently, his voice calm yet resolute.

"All right, let's get this over with", Ian's jaw tightened, his eyes reflecting a mixture of determination and apprehension.

Robert reached into his pocket, retrieved a key card, and swiped it through the card reader next to the door. A heavy click reverberated through the corridor as the door unlocked.

With a creaking sound, Robert the door open, revealing the spacious and clean shock room beyond.

The shock room was chillingly sterile, with white-tiled walls and a polished concrete floor. The room was well-lit, the fluorescent lights above casting an unwavering brightness. Along one wall, a row of menacing-looking machines and equipment stood ready for use.

At the centre of the room, a large metal chair, similar to the one in Simon's cell, was bolted to the floor, and upon it was Simon, a blacked-out mask covering his face. Thick leather restraints from its armrests and leg supports, designed to secure even the most resistant of inmates were holding Simon in one place. A tray of various tools, including electrodes and wires, sat nearby, waiting for their purpose to be fulfilled.

To the side of the chair, a two-way mirror allowed observers to watch without being seen. Behind the mirror, an observation room housed monitors, controls, and a small team of specialized officers ready to initiate the process.

"This room... it's a haunting reminder of how far we were willing to go for the truth" Ian spoke in a low voice. He took a deep breath, his eyes scanning the room with a mix of trepidation and a sense of duty.

"I can't believe this place even existed. The things they did in here..." Roni stopped in the middle of the sentence. Her voice filled with unease. Robert sensed her discomfort and placed a reassuring hand on Roni's shoulder.

"We couldn't change the past, but we ensured that we utilized this room responsibly. Our objective was to obtain information, not to cause unnecessary pain" he said softly.

"Let's do what we came here to do. We'll stay focused and minimize the harm inflicted. We need him alive after this" Ian said and took a step towards the chair.

The three of them took a collective breath, knowing that the decisions made within this room would forever shape the path of their investigation. The heavy door closed behind them, sealing them within the chilling confines of the shock room.

As the door closed behind them, the atmosphere in the shock room became more oppressive. The room seemed charged with tension, heavy with the weight of past actions and the uncertainty of the future. The environment inside was making Roni's insides scream. The shock room was a witness to the most horrific and painful sights in extracting truth from a criminal and the eeriness was thick in the air, the silence, deafening.

Ian, Roni, and the Robert near the imposing metal chair which held Simon. Ian took a moment to survey the surroundings, his gaze sweeping over the clinical white walls and the gleaming instruments of interrogation. A shiver ran down his spine as he contemplated the dark history of this room.

"Remember, our purpose here is to extract vital information. We must remain focused and committed to obtaining the truth while minimizing harm as much as possible", Ian said in a whisper so Simon could not hear them. His initial reaction to seeing Simon was pretty violent and they all hoped that Simon was not thinking that they will go soft on him.

Roni nodded, her eyes reflecting a mix of thrill and unease.

"We got this Chief. I will make him sing like a canary" the Robert winking at them.

They approached the chair, the leather restraints glistening under the harsh lights. The Robert the mask off Simon's head and gestured to Ian toward the observation room. "Let's move to the observation room. We'll initiate the process from there and monitor him."

"Monitor me? Why don't you go monitor your mother where she goes and what she does you greasy piece of shit?" Simon said as soon as he heard Robert talk.

"Thanks for giving me the motivation to fry your brains," Robert said smiling so positively that it was almost psychotic.

Simon who was dozing in and out of consciousness until then did not know he was in the shock room. He jerked his head and tried to get out of the seat before scanning the shock room. As soon as he realized where he was he started hurling profanities at everything in existence.

The three of them walked away and stepped through the adjacent doorway, entering the observation room, where a bank of monitors displayed different angles of the shock room. A specialized officer stood by alone, his eyes fixed on the screens, ready to intervene if necessary.

Ian's gaze turned to the main monitor, which showed Simon seated in the metal chair, surrounded by a chilling ambiance shaking violently.

Ian and Robert took their place at the control panel with Ian's hands steady as he prepared to initiate the interrogation. Ian and Roni exchanged a determined look, silently acknowledging their commitment to justice. Ian's finger hovered above the control panel, a mixture of reluctance and resolve coursing through his veins.

"Let's begin," Ian said without hesitation. "Shock the monkey," he said under his breath and pressed a button, and started talking.

"Simon Grunfeld, give us the name of your accomplice. We will ask twice if you live to see your pathetic cell" Ian said and took his finger off the button only to press the other button to send shocks to his chair.

The room came alive with a low hum of electricity. The instruments of interrogation buzzed to life, their eerie presence a stark reminder of the task at hand. As the process began, Ian looked at the monitors that displayed Simon's reaction, his body tensing and writhing under the weight of the electrical current.

Ian's jaw tightened, a pang of guilt tugging at his conscience. He focused on the screen, searching for any sign that their actions were leading to the breakthrough they desperately sought.

He looked at the specialized officer who was overseeing the interrogation who was not looking like he was going to stop anytime soon. Simon was shaking so hard that it felt like he was going to pop like a meat balloon.

Gritting his teeth Ian pressed the button again to stop electrocuting Simon and spoke on the mic after giving Simon to compose his senses.

"Simon Grunfeld. Name your accomplice!" Ian said.

Simon spat on the ground his eyes bloodshot. "Your moth..." Ian pressed the button again before Simon could complete the sentence. Simon's body was fed with electric current until Ian repeated the question again but Simon was not complying.

Time seemed to stretch as the interrogation unfolded, each passing moment filled with both anticipation and dread. The tension in the room grew, the echoes of past interrogations lingering in the air.

Roni glanced at Ian, her eyes reflecting concern and empathy. She reached out and gently placed a hand on his shoulder, offering silent support amidst the emotional turmoil.

Finally, after what felt like an eternity, the process concluded and Simon finally spoke.

"No more" The room fell silent as Simon, exhausted and battered, slumped in the chair. Robert took a deep breath and smiled at Ian and Roni.

Ian nodded, his gaze still fixed on the monitors, grappling with conflicting emotions. He spoke on the mic.

"Give us the…" Ian was interrupted in the middle of the sentence, "Samuel!" Simon said crying. "Samuel Grunfeld, my twin brother"

In the observation room, the team watched with a sombre understanding of the difficult choices made in the name of justice and the fruit it bore. Their eyes were wide with shock as the investigation took an unbelievable turn. "We got him!" Roni said clapping her hands. Ian bowed his head down on the control panel and took a deep breath as Simon cried in the background.

It was a summer afternoon in South Dakota. Logan Johnson, an aging mechanic with a wiry and skinny frame, stood in the garage, surrounded by the familiar sights and sounds of his work. He wiped the sweat from his brow, taking a momentary break from the repairs he was conducting. It was then that he noticed a colorful kite caught in the branches of a nearby tree.

A young boy, his eyes filled with hope, approached Logan, his voice filled with innocence.

"Hey Mister Johnson, can you help me get my kite down? It's stuck in the tree" he asked politely. Logan's tired eyes lit up with a warm smile as he looked at the young boy.

"Sure thing, kid. I'll get your kite back for you," Logan said affectionately.

Without hesitation, Logan's agile form moved swiftly toward the tree. He assessed the situation, his experienced eyes calculating the best approach. With remarkable agility, he began to climb the tree, his movements akin to that of a nimble monkey.

Branch by branch, he ascended, gracefully manoeuvring through the foliage until he reached the kite. Expertly, he hung onto one branch with a firm grip, freeing the kite from the other. With a gentle hand, he carefully untangled the string.

As Logan descended from the tree, his feet finding secure footing on each branch, he carried the kite in his hand. The young boy's face lit up with delight and gratitude as Logan handed the kite back to him.

"Wow, thank you so much! You're the best!" the young boy said excitedly.

"You're welcome, kid. Take care of that kite, all right?" said Logan softly.

The young boy nodded enthusiastically and quickly ran off, his kite soaring behind him. Logan chuckled, his worn face crinkling with a hint of nostalgia.

As Logan turned his gaze back towards the garage, his eyes caught sight of the television screen placed on a nearby shelf. His heart skipped a beat as he saw an all-too-familiar image—himself, hand-cuffed and sitting through a trial. The lines of time etched on the side of his eyes deepened, reflecting the weight of his past.

A mix of emotions flooded Logan's mind—shock, fear, and a haunting familiarity. The person on the screen was undeniably him, and they shared a connection from a time he had long tried to bury.

Chapter 9

The abandoned building loomed before them, a haunting structure filled with shadows and secrets. Detective Ian sat on the curb outside, his weary eyes scanning the scene, while the distant wail of ambulances and police sirens created an eerie symphony in the background. Officers rushed in and out of the building, their determined expressions painted with urgency.

Beside him, a junior officer sat, her body tense with shock and adrenaline. Her hands trembled slightly as she tried to process the intense experience she had just gone through. Ian noticed her distress and put a reassuring hand on her shoulder. He took a puff from a cigarette he had just lit and offered it to the shaking girl sitting next to him.

"Here, this will help," he said in a sympathetic tone.

"I do not smoke," said the girl stuttering.

"You did a great job today. That was very noble of you. The kid is safe and her family is grateful to you, they want to meet you," Ian said.

"Not tonight, I do not know if I will ever bounce back from this," she said looking at Ian with tired eyes.

"Take a deep breath officer," he said gently. "It was a tough operation, but you did well in there. You should be proud of yourself."

She nodded, her voice shaky as she responded, "I know, but... I've never been through anything like that before."

"I understand," Ian replied, his tone compassionate. "We encounter dark and unsettling things in our line of work, but it's what makes us stronger as officers."

Veronica took a deep breath, trying to steady herself. "It's just... it brings back memories of my childhood. This abandoned building reminds me of the rundown places I grew up around. The memories of my parents' passing and my brother's choices... it is all connected. It is like a sick game universe is playing with me."

Ian looked at her with empathy, knowing the weight she carried on her shoulders. "I can't imagine how tough it must be for you. Losing your parents at a young age and living in a tough neighborhood with your brother, Aaron."

Her eyes welled up with tears, but she tried to hold them back. "I always thought becoming a police officer would make a difference that I could protect people like my brother but I couldn't protect him. Aaron... he went down a dark path. I tried to get him to stop his illegal activities, but he just grew distant and bitter."

"You can't blame yourself for his choices," Ian said firmly. "People make their own decisions, and sometimes, no matter how hard we try, we can't change them. You had the strength to choose a different path, to become an honest officer and protect others."

She wiped away a tear, appreciating Ian's support. "Thank you, Ian. It's just hard to let go of the guilt sometimes."

"You're not alone in this, Veronica" Ian assured her.

"We're a team, and we support each other. Lean on me or any of your fellow officers whenever you need it. You have a long way to go and I see limitless potential in you. We've all been through tough times. That is what makes us who we are" he added thinking about his own demons in the process.

The junior officer sitting next to Ian on the curb was Veronica Smith. She was a woman of conviction, determined to make a difference in her community as an honest police officer. Her childhood had been tough, growing up in a neighborhood without her parents. Her older brother, Aaron, took on the role of caretaker after their parents tragically passed away when Veronica was just ten years old.

Living with Aaron wasn't easy; he worked at a pet shop, but the meager income wasn't enough to support them both. Fueled by desperation, he eventually fell into the dark embrace of a gang that dealt drugs and engaged in kidnapping for ransom. Veronica was devastated by her brother's choices and tried countless times to convince him to abandon his illegal activities, but her pleas fell on deaf ears, leaving her feeling heartbroken and distant from the only family she had left.

One day, as Veronica was diligently patrolling the neighborhood, she received a call from a distressed neighbor. Her neighbor's son had vanished without a trace, and Veronica sensed that something was amiss. She couldn't shake the feeling that her brother might be involved, but she needed evidence to act.

Veronica discreetly investigated and gathered enough information to confirm her fears: Aaron was behind the kidnapping. The innocent child was being held captive on the rooftop of an abandoned building, left to endure fear and dehydration.

Filled with conflicting emotions, Veronica knew she had to do the right thing, regardless of the personal toll it might take. She called for backup, alerting her fellow officers to the dire situation, and took it upon herself to confront her brother and rescue the child.

Arriving at the abandoned building, Veronica's heart pounded in her chest. The sirens wailed in the distance, a constant reminder of the urgency of the situation. Climbing the stairwell to the rooftop, she steeled herself for the confrontation ahead.

As she reached the top, the sight before her sent shivers down her spine. Aaron stood menacingly in front of the frightened child, who appeared weak and on the brink of collapse due to dehydration.

Veronica's heart pounded in her chest as she stood on the rooftop, her gun still raised. The sound of sirens grew louder, signaling the arrival of backup, but she knew she couldn't wait any longer. The life of an innocent child hung in the balance, and she had to act.

"Step away from the kid, Aaron!" Veronica's voice trembled with emotion, her eyes locked onto her brother. She hoped against hope that some part of him would listen to reason.

Aaron's smirk grew wider, his eyes filled with anger and bitterness. "Oh, now you're one of them, huh? You're going to shoot your own blood? Go ahead!"

Veronica's hands shook, torn between her duty as a police officer and her love for her brother. "You don't have to do this, Aaron. I can make it right. Just hand over the kid and walk away. I won't repeat myself."

"What did you say?" Aaron's voice dripped with venom. "I don't take orders from a pig, and if you've got a gun, I've got one too." He aimed his weapon at the terrified child, his finger dangerously close to the trigger. "This kid is a goner, and his blood is on you. I would've let him go after his old man paid me the protection money, but now I have to kill him."

Veronica's mind raced, searching for any possible solution. She knew she couldn't let her brother harm the child, but shooting him was tearing her apart inside. In a split-second decision, she steeled her resolve. She fired a shot, hitting Aaron on the right side of his chest, causing him to stagger back, but he remained standing.

Gritting her teeth, Veronica fired again, this time hitting him in the shoulder, making him lose his grip on the gun. As he stumbled backward, he lost his footing and fell off the edge of the building, falling on Veronica's car, crushing it under the weight of his now lifeless body.

The deafening silence that followed was only broken by the distant sirens growing nearer. Detective Ian arrived on the rooftop, his expression a mix of concern and relief as he saw Veronica comforting the terrified child.

"Veronica, are you all right?" Ian asked, his voice gentle as he approached her.

Veronica's hands trembled, her eyes locked on the rooftop's edge where her brother had fallen. "I... I had to do it, Sir. He left me no choice."

Ian placed a comforting hand on her shoulder. "You did what you had to do, Veronica. You saved that child's life."

Veronica's voice quivered as she tried to process what had just happened. "I never thought it would come to this. I tried so hard to get through to him, to make him see reason, but he just... he refused to listen."

"I know it's not easy," Ian said, his voice filled with empathy. "Sometimes, no matter how much we care for someone, we can't change their path. You did your best, and you made the right call in that moment to protect the innocent."

Veronica nodded, tears streaming down her cheeks. "I just wish there was another way, another outcome."

"We can't always control the outcome, Veronica," Ian said softly. "But we can control our actions and the choices we make. You did what you had to do as an officer, and I'm proud of you for that."

As the backup team arrived and secured the scene, Ian escorted Veronica and the kid downstairs, while comforting the scared kid and providing any assistance he could. His mind was in turmoil, torn between grief for Veronica's brother and relief that the child was safe.

In the days that followed, Veronica went through a range of emotions, from guilt to acceptance. She attended counseling sessions to help cope with the trauma she had experienced, but she knew it would take time to heal fully.

Her colleagues rallied around her, supporting her every step of the way. They understood the difficult position she had been in, and their unwavering support helped Veronica find strength in her darkest moments.

Veronica never forgot her brother, and the memories of their shared past haunted her. But she knew she had made the right choice that day on the rooftop, and she vowed to continue being an honest police officer, protecting the innocent and upholding the law.

Life had taken a toll on Veronica Smith. The incident with her brother Aaron had left scars that ran deep, and she found it difficult to let anyone get close to her. Her once warm and caring nature had now been replaced with a sense of detachment and coldness. She threw herself into her work, using her position as a police officer to focus on making a difference in the world, just as her parents had always wanted for her.

Despite her emotional barriers, Veronica found solace in her dedication to her job. Her fellow officers stood by her, supporting her every step of the way. They knew the struggles she had faced and admired her unwavering commitment to justice.

As the days turned into weeks, Veronica began to feel a faint glimmer of hope rekindling within her. The resilience she had developed from her challenging upbringing served as a guiding light, pushing her forward into an uncertain future. She was determined to be a beacon of hope, even in a world filled with darkness.

One day as the sun bathed the city streets in a warm glow, Detective Ian approached Officer Veronica, who was busy organizing some paperwork in her patrol car. He couldn't help but smile as he saw her cheerful demeanor, her dedication to her job shining through in every aspect.

"Hi Officer, how have you been?" Ian greeted her in a cheery tone as he approached.

Veronica looked up, her eyes lighting up with delight at seeing her colleague and friend. "Kicking ass and taking names Detective, how about you?" she responded playfully.

Ian chuckled at her response. "I am not too bad myself. I got some good news, and I had to see you as soon as I could," he said, extending his hand, which held an envelope.

"What is this?" Veronica asked, curiosity piqued, as she received the envelope and eagerly opened it.

As she read the contents, her wide eyes turned into shock, her hands trembling with emotion. The words on the paper held life-changing news, and tears began to well up in her eyes.

"Your track record is impressive Veronica. The police admires your courage. It takes a lot of effort to stand up to your foes and takes even more courage to stand up to your family. What you did made waves in the department, and I took the liberty of suggesting your name to the D.A.'s office," Ian said, his voice filled with admiration.

Veronica continued to read the words on the paper, her mind trying to process the enormity of what was happening. "In the light of your actions and your service and loyalty to

LAPD, you are being appointed as a senior detective at the D.A.'s office with all the amenities and a significant raise," Ian said, his tone cheerful.

Veronica was overwhelmed with emotions, unable to find the right words. She looked at Ian, her eyes glistening with tears. "I cannot believe this. You did this?" she managed to say, her voice filled with gratitude.

"Do not thank me, Veronica. You deserve all of this. We are proud of you," Ian said, patting her on the back.

As Veronica read the paper again and again, trying to absorb the reality of her promotion, Ian pointed across the street. Veronica followed his gaze, and her eyes widened in surprise and disbelief.

"Not only this. This job comes with a gift from all of us at the department" Ian said pointing across the street.

Standing there was a black, shining Cadillac. Veronica couldn't believe her eyes. "It's mine?" she asked, her voice breaking as she tried to compose herself.

"All yours!" Ian replied, handing the keys over to her. "Come on, let's take a look," he added, ushering her toward the sleek black beauty.

The beautiful sleek black shining Cadillac sat gracefully under the shade of the majestic tree in front of the precinct, like a regal monarch surrounded by its loyal subjects. The sunlight filtering through the tree's leaves cast dappled patterns on the car's glossy exterior, enhancing its allure.

The car's sleek lines flowed effortlessly, accentuating its refined and timeless design. The black paint sparkled, mirroring the world around it, as if capturing glimpses of the bustling city and the precinct's activities.

Chrome accents adorned the front grille, catching the light with a subtle glimmer. The polished rims of the wheels added a touch of elegance, perfectly complementing the overall sophisticated appearance.

The Cadillac's windows, tinted just enough to lend an air of mystery, invited the imagination to wander, wondering about the person sitting inside and the stories the car held within its luxurious confines.

Veronica ran her hand along the smooth surface of the car, her heart fluttering with excitement. She opened the door and sat on the driver's seat, gripping the steering wheel tightly, taking in the luxurious interior.

As officers and civilians walked by, their gazes couldn't help but linger on the stunning car. It was a captivating sight, leaving an impression of power and sophistication on all who beheld it.

"You like it?" Ian asked sitting in the passenger seat, smiling at her reaction.

"I love it! Was this your idea?" Veronica inquired, her eyes shining with gratitude.

"Guilty as charged," Ian said, chuckling and raising his hand playfully. "What do you want to do now, Partner?" he asked.

"Say what?" Veronica explained.

"Yep, I told you. We are a team" Ian said smiling cheerfully.

Veronica's face lit up with a mischievous grin. "Let's take her for a spin!" she said with childish excitement.

"Ah yes, I could use a drop-off too. Step on it Roni!" Ian said, buckling up as Veronica revved the engine loud, the car's powerful purr filling the air. They drove off together, leaving the station behind, embarking on a new chapter in their professional career, filled with pride, joy, and the thrill of the open road. Since that day Roni and Ian were inseparable. They were a cohesive unit and they solved every case they laid their hands on. They were on their way to becoming legends and nothing could stop them.

As the sun began to set, casting a warm orange glow over the city, Roni and Ian found themselves in the precinct's conference room, going through the details of the case. The confession from Simon had taken them by surprise, unraveling the seemingly watertight case they had built against him. It was a sobering reminder that not everything was as it seemed.

Roni couldn't shake the feeling of empathy for Simon. The realization that he had spent two decades behind bars for a crime he didn't commit weighed heavily on her heart. She knew the pain of having to make a difficult decision, just as she had done with her own brother, Aaron. The memories of that fateful rooftop confrontation flooded back, the anguish of having to choose between family and justice resurfacing.

"It's unbelievable, Ian," Roni said, her voice tinged with frustration. "To think that someone could let their own twin brother suffer for their actions... it's beyond comprehension."

Ian nodded solemnly, understanding the turmoil that Roni must be feeling. "It's a harsh reality, but unfortunately, it happens," he replied. "Sometimes, people are driven by their own selfish motives, even at the expense of their loved ones."

Roni clenched her fists, the memory of Aaron's sneering face on that rooftop still haunting her. "I can't help but think about my brother," she admitted, her voice breaking slightly. "I tried to reason with him, to save him from his own darkness, but he chose a path that led to destruction."

Ian placed a reassuring hand on Roni's shoulder. "You did what you had to do," he said gently. "As a police officer, your duty is to protect the innocent, regardless of who they may be related to. It's never an easy choice, but you showed immense courage and integrity that day."

Roni nodded, appreciating Ian's understanding and support. "I just wish Simon's brother would have had the same conscience," she said, her jaw tightening with resolve. "I won't rest until we find Samuel and bring him to justice for what he's done. This has become personal."

"We'll do everything in our power to make that happen," Ian assured her, his eyes filled with determination. "We won't let Simon's sacrifice go in vain."

As the night wore on, Roni and Ian continued to delve into the case, tirelessly working to uncover the truth and track down Samuel. Their partnership had become more than just professional; they had formed a deep bond that extended beyond the precinct's walls.

"All right Roni, I am done for the night," Ian said getting up.

"Let me drop you home Chief," Roni said grabbing her keys.

"It is all right. I will have a patrol car drop me home, you take care all right?" Ian said wearing his jacket.

"If you say so. Take care" Roni said.

Ian head out in the night and besides taking the patrol car he decided to walk. The rain had stopped and a chilly air was blowing. He lit up a cigarette and walked toward his apartment which was a few blocks down the road. As he walked he thought about his own life. He smiled at the thought of the breakthrough they got in Simon's case and enjoyed his cigarette with a satisfied expression on his face.

As he entered his apartment he felt loneliness creeping up. He walked through the corridor toward the fridge to get a beer. The dimly lit apartment seemed to echo with the silence of loneliness as Ian sank into the worn-out sofa, the weight of his solitude settling heavily upon his shoulders. The rain had ceased, leaving behind a hauntingly cold breeze that seemed to seep into the very core of his being.

He took a deep drag from his cigarette, the smoke swirling around him like a desperate plea for comfort. The taste of bitterness on his lips matched the ache in his heart, a poignant reminder of the emptiness he carried within.

As he walked through the corridor adorned with pictures of his past, his once bright eyes now held a glimmer of sadness. The photos displayed moments frozen in time - laughter, love, and happiness that now felt like distant memories. Among them were pictures of him with his wife, a woman he once loved deeply, but whom he had inadvertently pushed away with his unyielding dedication to his work.

He longed for her presence, her touch, and her warmth, but those were mere fragments of a life he had lost. The walls seemed to whisper the echoes of their arguments, each word a reminder of the cracks that had formed in their relationship.

The television flickered in the background, offering a feeble attempt to distract himself from the emptiness. The noise from the screen blended with the sounds of his own thoughts, creating a cacophony of emotions that he struggled to drown out.

The beer in his hand brought little solace, its taste bitter like the memories that plagued him. Each sip was an attempt to numb the pain, to quiet the yearning for human connection that had become a constant ache.

As the night wore on, Ian's eyes grew heavy with exhaustion. He knew that sleep would bring no respite; instead, it would lead to dreams haunted by what ifs and what could have beens. He welcomed the darkness that enveloped him, as it offered a temporary escape from the harsh reality of his life.

Loneliness had become his companion, and it seemed to follow him wherever he went. The success in his career, the camaraderie with Roni, all faded into insignificance when faced with the overwhelming emptiness that engulfed him.

He closed his eyes, seeking solace in the temporary oblivion of sleep. But even in slumber, his dreams were tinged with melancholy, a stark reminder of the void that loomed within his soul.

In the silence of the night, Ian lay on the sofa, a shadow of the man he once was. The world outside moved on, oblivious to the quiet pain that resided in his heart.

As the hours ticked by, he knew that another day would bring the same routine - the facade of strength and purpose during the day, followed by the all-consuming loneliness of the night.

At that moment, Ian felt like a ship adrift on a vast ocean, with no harbor in sight. And as he slept, loneliness remained his constant companion, a loyal friend in a world that seemed to have forgotten him.

Chapter 10

The cloudy day did little to dampen Ian's spirits as he woke up feeling a bit light-headed. He shook off the grogginess and proceeded with his usual morning routine. A refreshing shower helped clear his mind, and he got dressed, ready to face whatever the day had in store for him.

Ian had a regular routine of starting his day at a local diner, a place he frequented for a cup of coffee to kickstart his mornings. As he entered, he was greeted by the warm smile of Stephanie, one of the waitresses. She wasted no time in bringing him his usual cup of coffee, her cheerful demeanor setting a positive tone for his day.

With coffee in hand, Ian found a seat at a table to enjoy his morning cup. He didn't have to wait long for company as his partner, Roni, walked in, greeting him with a friendly "Hey, chief."

"Hey there!" Ian replied with a smile, gesturing to Stephanie to bring another cup of coffee for Roni. Stephanie sashayed over, playfully chewing gum as she set the fresh cup down in front of Roni. Ian couldn't help but notice how

Stephanie's eyes seemed to linger on him, her demeanor almost flirtatious.

Roni picked up on the waitress's behavior and took a sip of her coffee, arching an eyebrow playfully. "What's the deal with her?" she asked, nodding towards Stephanie.

Ian chuckled, taking a sip of his own coffee. "I put her husband in jail for grand theft auto. Since he's behind bars, she seems to be extremely grateful to me," he explained.

Roni smirked, her eyes gleaming mischievously. "She looks at you like you're a juicy steak," she remarked, teasingly.

Ian laughed, finding humor in the situation. "Well, let's just say she's quite fond of her morning coffee," he replied with a wink.

As they savored their breakfast, the conversation shifted to business. Roni wanted to know their next move in catching Samuel, their elusive target.

"So what now, chief? How do we catch this Samuel?" Roni asked, her tone serious and focused.

Ian leaned back in his chair, a thoughtful expression on his face. "Actually, we don't have to catch him," he said nonchalantly.

Roni's eyebrows shot up in surprise. "What do you mean? We can't just let him roam free," she argued.

A confident smile played on Ian's lips. "We'll draw him out," he stated cryptically.

"But how? He's been elusive for so long," Roni questioned, her curiosity piqued.

Ian's gaze locked with hers, a glint of determination in his eyes. "You leave that to me," he replied, his tone full of assurance.

After coffee, Ian and Roni made their way to their office. As Ian sat in his office, his mind racing with possibilities. He had a feeling that there was more to the recent robberies than met the eye, and now that he knew there was another person involved, he was determined to unravel the truth.

"We will make him famous!" Ian exclaimed excitedly, a glint of determination in his eyes. Roni looked at him with a mix of curiosity and concern, wondering what he had in mind.

"Who do you mean?" she asked, eager to understand Ian's plan.

"This guy Samuel or his accomplice, whoever is behind these robberies. They want attention; they want to be found. They've been challenging us at every turn and putting on a show. We'll give them what they want, and we'll see them squirm," Ian explained, his voice tinged with both excitement and shrewdness.

Roni raised an eyebrow, intrigued by Ian's approach. "You want to provoke them?" she clarified.

"Precisely!" Ian replied, a hint of mischief in his smile. "If they have a short temper, we'll use that to our advantage. We'll strike their nerves, and we'll see how they react when the tables are turned."

Roni nodded, beginning to see the logic in Ian's plan. She knew that their elusive target was taunting them, challenging their abilities at every turn. But Ian had an idea to flip the script, to taunt the taunter, and see what emerged from the shadows.

"But how do we strike their nerves?" Roni asked, curious about the specific tactics they would employ.

Ian leaned back in his chair, a confident expression on his face. "We use our intelligence and resources," he replied. "We start digging deeper, following the breadcrumbs they've left behind. We uncover their past, their secrets, and then we use that knowledge to rattle them."

Roni nodded, beginning to see the brilliance in Ian's plan. If they could find the right triggers, they might be able to get under their target's skin, pushing them to make mistakes or reveal themselves in a moment of frustration.

As they continued to discuss their strategy, Ian began formulating a plan to strike back at their elusive foe. He knew it would be a delicate game, one that required finesse and precision. But he was confident that they could outwit their adversary and turn the tables on them.

Days turned into weeks as Ian and Roni carefully laid the groundwork for their retaliation. They gathered every piece of information they could find, analyzing patterns and behaviors, and seeking out any vulnerabilities they could exploit.

Finally, the time had come to put their plan into action. Ian and Roni orchestrated a series of events, leaving subtle clues and hints for their target to find. They strategically leaked information, making it seem like they were getting closer to solving the case.

As they waited for their adversary's response, tension hung in the air. They knew they were playing a dangerous game, and the stakes were high. But Ian was confident that they had the upper hand.

"What is this? I am seeing you there smiling and laughing! Are you setting me up!" Samuel said over the phone while looking out the window. He was clearly paranoid. He had turned all of the lights off in his house and locked the door from outside making it look like no one was home while his revolver was laying in front of him on the table with half bottle of whiskey.

The tension in Samuel's voice was palpable as he spoke frantically over the phone. He was clearly on edge, feeling like he was being set up. Paranoid and anxious, he had taken extreme measures to fortify his home, creating the illusion that he wasn't there. His revolver lay on the table in front of him, a symbol of his desperation and fear.

On the other end of the line, Samantha tried to calm her accomplice down, her voice laced with frustration. "Those detectives are just playing mind games with you, okay? Keep it together! No one is coming for you," she assured him, her teeth clenched in irritation.

Samuel's fear seemed to intensify, but he tried to trust Samantha's words. He knew he was in deep, and the weight of their actions was beginning to take a toll on his sanity.

"I don't know. I feel like they're everywhere. Watching me. Waiting to pounce," he whispered, his eyes darting around the dimly lit room.

"Listen to me, old man. You need to stay calm and think rationally. I've been careful, and they have no solid evidence against you," Samantha replied, trying to reassure him.

Meanwhile, at Samantha's house, William was sound asleep, blissfully unaware of the sinister activities his wife was involved in. Samantha kept her voice low, not wanting to wake him. Her heart raced as she continued to talk to Samuel, her mind occupied with both her husband and their dangerous situation.

"You did what you had to do with your husband, right? He won't know a thing," Samuel asked anxiously.

Samantha sighed, trying to suppress her guilt. "Yeah, I took care of him. He won't. Just focus on laying low," she said, her voice tinged with regret.

As the conversation continued, Samantha couldn't help but feel the weight of the lies and deception she had woven. She had delved deeper into a world she never imagined, and the consequences were far greater than she had ever anticipated.

Back at Samuel's house, he took a deep swig of whiskey, trying to calm his nerves. He knew he was in a dangerous game, and one wrong move could cost him everything. But Samantha's assurances provided a semblance of comfort, and he tried to believe that they would emerge unscathed.

The room was filled with tension as Samuel's anger boiled over. He couldn't believe how quickly everything had fallen apart, and he was growing increasingly frustrated with their predicament. He threw his whiskey glass across the room, the sound of shattering glass echoing in the air.

"Keep it together, Sam!" Samantha urged, trying to maintain her composure despite the mounting pressure.

"They've plastered my face everywhere! They're even dragging my family into this mess! My mother doesn't deserve this," Samuel lamented, feeling the weight of his actions bearing down on him.

Samantha understood his distress but remained firm in her resolve. "They're manipulating the media, Sam. It's a tactic to gain public sympathy and make themselves look like the heroes. Don't let their propaganda get to you," she advised.

Samuel couldn't help but feel helpless as he saw the news coverage, exposing his identity to the world. He watched in disbelief as his twin brother, Simon, sat with the police, playing his part in the drama that had unfolded.

"They're making it impossible for me to lay low!" Samuel exclaimed, his frustration mounting. "And you! Giving press conferences and being seen all over the place! Don't you realize that puts me at risk?"

Samantha tried to reason with him, understanding his concern. "I had to play their game, Sam. We need to control the narrative. It's the only way to counter their lies and protect ourselves," she explained.

"Look, it's on now! Look at it!" Samuel exclaimed, his voice tinged with desperation.

Samantha turned the television on, and there it was, the face of Simon, Samuel's twin brother, filling the screen. A female voice narrated his tragic life story, recounting the crimes he was being questioned for. Samuel couldn't tear his eyes away from the screen, his heart pounding in his chest.

"In a world that was once filled with promise and potential, there lived a man named Simon. He was once a banker, navigating complex financial landscapes with ease and precision. But as fate would have it, his life took a dark and tragic turn.

Simon had a twin brother, Samuel, and together, they were inseparable. Two halves of a whole, they navigated life side by side, sharing a bond that seemed unbreakable. But beneath the surface of their seemingly ordinary lives, a world of darkness was lurking, waiting to consume them.

It all began innocently enough - a simple act of desperation that led to a path they could never return from.

One brother fell into a world of theft and deception, his desperate choices driven by a desire to escape the harsh realities that life had thrown his way.

As the days turned into nights, his crimes escalated, leaving a trail of chaos and destruction in his wake. What once was mere survival turned into a sinister thirst for power and control. The lines between right and wrong blurred, and he was consumed by a darkness that knew no bounds.

His crimes knew no limits, and the depths of his depravity seemed endless. Murder became just another tool in his arsenal, as he clawed his way further into the abyss of criminality.

But in the cruel twist of fate, it was Simon who found himself behind bars, paying the price for the sins his twin brother had committed. As he faced the consequences of his actions, he couldn't help but wonder how he had arrived at this point, trapped in a world he had never intended to inhabit.

Meanwhile, Samuel remained free, lurking in the shadows, evading justice with a cunning prowess that seemed unmatched. He may be roaming free now, but we will get him soon," Roni declared standing on the podium, her voice filled with resolve.

The footage shifted to another video, and Samantha's face appeared on the screen. She was the District Attorney, and her confident demeanor couldn't be missed as she addressed the public. She spoke of catching Simon's accomplice and promised to reveal the name soon. Her words sent a chill down Samuel's spine.

"We've almost caught him," Samantha said, her voice echoing through the room. "The nationwide manhunt is in full swing."

Samuel couldn't believe what he was seeing and hearing. The reality of the situation was sinking in, and he knew he was in grave danger. His face was associated with the crimes, and he felt like a trapped animal, hunted and cornered.

The television screen changed, displaying a picture of Simon with the ominous title, "Most Wanted Man in America." Samuel's heart sank as he saw his name connected to such a damning label. It was a nightmare come to life, and he was paralyzed with fear.

Samantha felt trapped, she had a job to do, and that meant putting on a strong front for the public. But deep down, she knew the implications of her actions. She was torn between her duty and her corrupt relationship with Samuel.

As the news continued to unfold, Samuel's mind raced with thoughts of escape. He couldn't afford to be captured, not after what he had done to protect himself and his secret life. The whiskey provided a temporary escape from the reality of the situation, but it couldn't numb the fear that was gnawing at him.

"We have to do something," Samuel said, his voice shaky but determined. "I can't just sit here and wait for them to find me."

"Just lay low! I will contact you," Samantha said firmly, her voice laced with urgency. "I'm working on the new identity documents, and as soon as they're ready, I'll let you know."

Samuel, however, was growing impatient and desperate. He needed money to survive while he waited for his new identity, and the fear of being captured was gnawing at him. "I don't know about that. I want money because I'm running low. I want it tomorrow!" he demanded angrily.

Samantha understood his frustration, but she couldn't be swayed by his demands. "I won't be blackmailed like this for what I've done for you!" she retorted, pounding her fist on the table.

Deep down, Samantha knew that helping Samuel came with risks. She had already taken immense personal and professional risks to protect him, and now she was going even further to secure his safety. But she couldn't let his anger cloud her judgment.

Her plan was clear - get Samuel a new identity and provide him with enough money to start a new life in another country, away from the danger that was closing in on him.

The anger and frustration in the air were palpable as Samuel's demanding voice echoed through the phone. "I made you who you are, and you owe me," he declared, his tone unwavering.

But Samantha was not one to be cowed by his threats. "I don't owe anyone anything! You left me to rot!" she spat back, her voice seething with resentment. "I picked you up and gave you what you wanted! You were dead!" she added, her words laced with bitterness.

Their conversation was a bitter reminder of the dark history they shared. Samantha had once been down and out, a street rat with nothing to her name. But Samuel had taken her under his wing, telling her that he is her real father and giving her the opportunity to rise above her circumstances and become the successful District Attorney she was today.

But that past was marred with darkness, and Samantha couldn't forget how Samuel had manipulated her and involved her in a world of crime.

Samuel was relentless in his pursuit of what he believed was rightfully his. "All these riches and money are because of what I taught you," he argued. "You were nothing before me."

But Samantha had worked hard for her success, and she wasn't about to let him take credit for it. "I earned every bit of my success," she retorted. "You may have given me opportunities, but I made my own choices and worked hard to get to where I am."

"I want my money tomorrow or I will go to the police myself. They will be interested in a story about a D.A. turned murderer or a murderer turned D.A. whatever is more amusing to them and the press. Let's see how you act when you are on TV with the words 'Most Wanted' plastered on your face!" Samuel yelled on the phone before hanging up.

Frustration and desperation consumed Samantha. She knew that if Samuel went to the police, her carefully built life would crumble. The thought of her dark activities being exposed haunted her, and she felt trapped in a corner with nowhere to turn.

As she saw the faces of Ian and Roni on the screen her blood began to boil. She knew that desperate measures were necessary, and she was willing to do whatever it took to protect herself.

Chapter 11

As Ian and Roni made their way down the long, echoing hallway toward Simon's cell, they discussed their plans for the press conference and their strategy for locating Samuel.

"The press conference went pretty well; don't you think?" Ian said adjusting his tie.

"Yeah, it did. But we need to be careful about how much information we disclose. We don't want to jeopardize the investigation or put Simon's life at risk" Roni nodded.

"Agreed. We can't reveal everything, but we should give the public enough to generate some leads. The more eyes we have on this case, the better chance we have of finding Samuel," Ian said.

"Definitely. We'll have to emphasize the importance of Samuel's involvement in the recent heists and ask anyone with information to come forward anonymously," Roni said checking her notes.

"And during the Q&A session, we'll have to be on our toes. Reporters might try to dig deep into Simon's past, and we need to control the narrative," Ian said.

"Don't worry Chief. We'll handle it tactfully and redirect their focus back to the case," Roni said.

As they reached Simon's cell, they found him sitting on the narrow bed, looking alert. He looked better than he did before and he was shifted to a more spacious room at Ian's request to the C.O. Robert who was turning out to be a not-so-bad person after all.

The clinking of keys echoed as the guard unlocked the cell door, allowing Ian and Roni to step inside.

"Simon, we're back. How are you holding up?" Ian greeted him cheerfully.

"Hanging in there. Any news?" Simon said with a weary yet seemingly brighter smile.

"Not yet, but we're working on it. We want to talk to you about your brother," Roni said to Simon in a sympathetic tone. She could relate to how Simon must have felt and Ian told her that she is the best person to ask him about his brother.

"I told you what I know officers. He's been gone for years, and I have no idea where he could be hiding" Simon said his expression sad.

"We understand, Simon. But we're not giving up. We'll find a way; we just need to dig deeper, right, Chief?" said Roni to Ian.

"You think you can find him?" Simon said now smiling sarcastically.

"We'll do everything we can. Finding Samuel is crucial to cracking this case wide open. We believe he might be the key to unraveling the entire operation," Roni said nodding confidently.

"And if he's been involved in these recent heists, we need to get him off the streets. But we can't do it alone; we need your help" Ian said.

"You have my cooperation. I want to see my brother pay for what he's done, and if that means helping you find him, I'm all in," said Simon.

"Thank you, Simon. Your cooperation means a lot to us, and it will help bring justice to those affected by these crimes," Roni said appreciating Simon.

"Just hang in there, and we'll get through this together," Ian said his words firm.

The atmosphere was a little less tense now that there was a development made in the case after Simon was shocked to his senses. He was wearing an orange jumpsuit and looked cleaner.

"Simon, did you have your lunch today?" Ian said leaning forward.

"Yes, thank you. I appreciate that you guys asked Robert to take care of me. The food has been better lately," Simon said looking slightly surprised.

"It's the least we can do, Simon. We want to make sure you're being treated fairly during the investigation" Roni said in a soft tone.

"Now, let's talk about your twin brother, Samuel. Does he have a family except you?" Ian said coming back to the topic.

Simon took a look at Ian and Roni and sighed. "Samuel has had a rough time. His wife left him for another man, and it shattered him. After his last heist, he couldn't handle it anymore and just... vanished. Abandoned his daughter and fled."

"Wait, Samuel had a daughter?" Ian asked in a surprised tone.

"Yes, he did. Poor girl, he left her with me, so I adopted her as my own. But she never liked me much. And after I was imprisoned a few years ago, my wife told me that she ran away from home" Simon said his head hung low.

"That's heart-breaking. Do you have any idea where she might be?" Roni said in a concerned voice.

"No, I wish I did. Sometimes I wonder where she is and how she's doing. My poor Samantha" Simon said shaking his head.

Ian and Roni exchanged a glance, feeling sympathy for Simon's situation. For some reason, their hearts skipped a beat at the mention of the name Samantha. Their intuitions were loud and they could not wait to discuss this with each other after they are done with the interrogation.

"We'll do what we can to find her, Simon. But right now, we need to focus on the current situation" Ian said wrapping it up quickly.

"We'll be back to talk more later, and we'll try to locate your daughter too," Roni said nodding.

"Thank you, guys. I really appreciate your efforts," Simon said.

With that, Ian and Roni got up to leave the jail cell, their minds filled with both the current case and the new development about Simon's estranged daughter. Ian and Roni sat in the shiny black Cadillac, parked on a quiet street. The weight of the investigation and the silence inside the vehicle seemed almost suffocating. Finally, Roni broke the silence.

"So, Samantha" Roni spoke.

"Samantha Grundfeld" Ian said nodding.

"We know she holds the key to finding Samuel. We just need to figure out where she is" Roni said leaning forward.

"Agreed. Let's head back to the office and go through Samuel's files again. There must be some clue that we've missed" Ian said determination dripping through his words.

They drove back to their office, where stacks of files and evidence awaited them. Ian and Roni combed through the documents, searching for any link to Samantha Grundfeld.

"Look here! Samantha Grundfeld, it's mentioned in this document. It says she was adopted when she was 14 and attended a Catholic school" Ian said excitedly.

"That's right. She left home and ended up in a shelter home in Wisconsin" said Roni looking at the document in Ian's hand.

"No way!" Roni exclaimed causing Ian to spill his coffee a little.

"You scared me! What is it?" Ian asked.

"Chief! You are not going to believe this" Roni said her eyes wide in shock.

"Let me have a look at it," Ian said coming over to her and taking the document from her hand.

He could not believe what he saw. His intuitions were right from the start. He knew something was very wrong with this case and today he knew what.

On the document he held it was written that Samantha Grundfeld studied her way into a college and studied law to become the assistant D.A. She changed her name to 'Samantha Williams after she got married to William Katz.

Ian took the document from Roni's hand and read it again, disbelief spreading across his face. Everything suddenly started to make sense.

"I knew it! My instincts were right from the beginning. There was something off about this case, and now we know what it is" Ian said his fist balling.

"Why did not the D.A. tell us about this? Simon had a twin brother and she knew that all along. Samuel is her father!" Roni said in a furious tone.

"Exactly. We need to approach this delicately. Let's gather more information on Samantha Williams now. We are close!" Ian said gritting his teeth and lighting up a cigarette.

"Agreed, Chief. This could be the breakthrough we've been waiting for" Roni said.

"This is Roni. This is" Ian said inhaling deeply.

Ian and Roni knew they were on the right track. Samantha Grundfeld, now Samantha Williams, was the key to finding Samuel and uncovering the truth behind the heists. They were ready to take the next steps in their investigation and bring this case to a close. Their next lead was the D.A. herself.

William Katz, a respectable businessman who owned several casinos in Las Vegas, sat behind his desk in his office, engrossed in his work. He was a huge man with a calm personality and a bald head.

His secretary Stacy entered the room, holding a file, and leaned over the desk, attempting to capture his attention. Sensing her advances, Katz remained focused on his business and didn't even bother to look up.

"Here are the statements, Mr. Katz. Do you need anything else?" she asked, her voice dripping with flirtation.

Without lifting his gaze from the documents in front of him, Katz replied, "No, that will be all. I am expecting Detective Ian. Is he here yet?"

The secretary confirmed, "Yes, he's sitting outside. Would you like me to send him in?"

Katz nodded, still immersed in his work. "Yes, please do. And also, get two coffees for us. Take the rest of the day off."

As she left the room, Katz set aside his work and prepared to meet Detective Ian from the LAPD. Moments later, a knock on the door signaled the detective's arrival. William invited him in, rising from his seat to shake Ian's hand.

"Detective Ian, a pleasure to meet you. Please, have a seat," William said, gesturing to the chair across from his desk.

Ian settled into the chair and engaged in small talk, asking about the state of Katz's business. Katz proudly explained how the influx of tourists and gamblers had led to a flourishing industry in Las Vegas.

Ian chuckled lightly and remarked, "And so is the crime rate, Mr. Katz."

Katz sighed and replied, "Oh, yes, especially after that stolen violin incident. I hope you guys catch that son of a bitch soon."

Curious about Katz's choice of words, Ian asked, "Why couldn't it be a woman? Why does everybody always say 'son of a bitch'?"

Taken aback, Katz responded, "What do you mean? Are you suggesting that the person behind these crimes is a woman? That seems impossible."

Ian leaned back in his chair, studying William intently. "Women are stronger and more cunning than you might think, Mr. Katz. When they set their sights on something, they can be relentless. If they have the motivation, they are capable of going to extreme lengths to achieve their goals."

Considering Ian's words, Katz mused, "Well, perhaps you're right."

"Take your wife as an example. She is doing a swell job as a D.A. She is a clever and strong woman I must say, the likes of which are rarely seen" Ian added.

"Yes, she is but what does she have to do with this? She is spending days and nights immersed in this case of yours" Katz said squinting his eyes in confusion.

Ian's expression turned serious as he pushed a file across the desk toward Katz. As he read its contents, William's shock grew.

"Detective, this is utter nonsense! Are you here to insult me and accuse my wife, who is a respected District Attorney? Are you after her position? Who put you up to this?" William said his expressions furious.

Ian remained calm in the face of William's anger. "Mr. Katz, please calm down. I'm not here to insult you or your wife. I'm here to bring the truth to light. Your wife is indeed working on the case, but the truth is, she is not solving it—she is misleading us."

Furious, Katz stood up, his voice rising. "This is outrageous! I am going to file a case against you for these false accusations!"

Ian's voice remained steady. "Mr. Katz, if you proceed with that, you will not only lose your case but your reputation and your precious casinos as well. We don't yet know if you are involved or not. If you are innocent and believe your wife is not the culprit, I suggest you investigate this matter for yourself before taking any rash actions."

Ian paused for a moment before continuing, "Samantha Williams was previously known as Samantha Grundfeld. Her father, Simon Grundfeld, is currently behind bars for similar crimes our case is linked to and her biological father who is a twin of Simon Grundfeld is on the run. I suggest you look into this information and let me know what you find."

Katz, torn between anger and confusion, sank back into his chair. He realized that the situation was more complex than he had initially assumed. He contemplated the weight of Ian's words and the implications they held for his wife and his own life.

Detective Ian leaned back in his chair, watching William Katz closely as he processed the shocking revelation. Katz sat across from him, his brow furrowed and his eyes wide with disbelief.

"I know this is a lot to take in," Ian said calmly, "but you need to think about it. Take a day or two if you need to. I understand that it's not easy to believe that your own wife could be involved in something like this."

Katz shook his head, trying to make sense of the information he had just learned. "I just can't believe it, Detective. We've been married for ten years, and I thought I knew her so well. How could she be involved in a criminal investigation?"

"It's not always easy to see what people are capable of," Ian replied sympathetically.

"Sometimes, they can be hiding a whole different side of themselves. That's why we're here, to uncover the truth."

Ian reached into his pocket and pulled out his business card. He handed it to Katz. "When you're ready to talk about it, give me a call. I'll be here to help you through this."

Katz took the card, studying it for a moment before looking back at Ian. "Thank you, Detective. I appreciate your understanding."

"Just remember," Ian said as he stood up from the chair, "we're here to find the truth, no matter where it leads us."

As he picked up his badge from the table, Katz's expression remained troubled. "Detective, what happens if it turns out she's involved? What will you do?"

Ian hesitated for a moment, choosing his words carefully. "If the evidence points in that direction, we'll have to pursue the investigation wherever it takes us. It won't be easy, but we have a duty to uphold the law and protect the innocent."

Katz nodded solemnly, realizing the gravity of the situation. "I understand."

As Ian made his way towards the door, he turned back to Katz one more time. "And please, do not tell your wife that we're investigating her. She's a powerful woman, and I don't want to get into trouble. I don't want to throw her name in public, so let's just keep it low, okay?"

Katz was taken aback by the request but nodded in agreement. "I won't say a word, Detective. I'll keep it to myself.

"Thank you," Ian said, appreciating Katz's understanding. "I know it's a lot to ask, but it's for the best at this point."

With that, Ian walked out of the room, leaving Katz to grapple with the information he had just received. As the door closed behind him, Katz's mind raced with questions and doubts. He had always thought of his wife as a strong, influential woman, but now he wondered if there was a darker side to her that he had never seen. The side that comes out when she was out late in the night.

Over the next few days, Katz took Ian's advice and tried to process the situation. He struggled with conflicting emotions, torn between his loyalty to his wife and his sense of duty to uncover the truth. Finally, unable to bear the burden alone, he decided to make the call he had been putting off.

Dialing the number on Ian's business card, Katz took a deep breath as he waited for the detective to pick up. When Ian's voice came through the line, Katz cleared his throat nervously.

"Detective Ian, it's William Katz. I need to talk to you about my wife."

Chapter 12

The stormy night cast an eerie atmosphere over the Pigeon Forge Museum in Las Vegas. Rain lashed against the windows, accompanied by distant rumbles of thunder. Inside the museum, two guards, Mike and Dave, huddled together in the security room, seeking solace from the tempest outside. Their steaming cups of coffee provided a comforting warmth as they exchanged creepy tales to pass the time.

Dave, a stout man with a greying beard, leaned back in his chair, his eyes darting around the dimly lit room. "You know, Mike, they say this place is haunted. People claim they've seen strange shadows moving through the corridors at night, even when no one's supposed to be here."

Mike, a younger guard with a skeptical look on his face, chuckled and took a sip of his coffee. "Come on, Dave, don't tell me you actually believe in all that supernatural stuff."

Dave grinned mischievously. "Believe it or not, my friend, some things just can't be explained. You'll think differently when you've been working here as long as I have."

The sound of rain tapping against the window intensified as Mike leaned closer, intrigued by Dave's cryptic remark. "All right, Dave, I'm all ears. Hit me with one of your creepy stories."

Dave leaned in, his voice dropping to a whisper. "All right, let me tell you about the legend of Old Man Jefferson. They say he was a twisted soul who loved to collect rare artifacts, even resorting to sinister means to acquire them."

Mike raised an eyebrow, curiosity piqued. "Sinister means? What are you talking about?"

Dave's eyes gleamed with excitement. "Legend has it that one stormy night, Old Man Jefferson was struck by lightning while attempting to steal the priceless violin. Since then, his restless spirit roams this museum, seeking vengeance on anyone who crosses his path."

Mike scoffed, though a slight shiver ran down his spine. "All right, that's enough. You've given me the chills. Let's just focus on our job."

Just as Mike said that he felt an urgent need to relieve himself and excused himself to the restroom. Dave, feeling drowsy from the combination of the stormy ambiance and the warmth of the room, reclined back in his chair, fighting off sleep.

Meanwhile, inside the museum's grand exhibition hall, a magnificent chandelier dangled from the ceiling, its crystals shimmering in the dim lighting. Unbeknownst to anyone, the chandelier's screws, which secured it to the roof, began to unscrew without a sound. Slowly, inch by inch, the chandelier descended, revealing a hidden rope that supported its weight.

Just as it seemed like the chandelier would plummet to the ground, shattering into a million pieces, it stopped a mere few feet from the polished marble floor. A mysterious figure, clad in sleek black attire, descended from the rope with unmatched grace. Landing silently on the ground, she moved with a sultry and stealthy gait, reminiscent of a feline stalking its prey.

The figure, her face obscured by a dark hood, made her way toward the centrepiece of the museum—the Nearly 300-Year-Old Guarneri Violin. With each step, she seemed to dance through the shadows, her movements fluid and captivating.

From a concealed pocket, the mysterious figure produced a glass cutter. With precision, she made a neat incision on the top of the glass case housing the priceless instrument. The room remained eerily silent, the security system oblivious to the impending theft.

As the glass fell away, the figure delicately lifted the Guarneri Violin, its aged wood gleaming in the faint light. A triumphant smile played across her lips as she murmured, "Bingo."

With the violin securely stowed in her backpack, the mysterious woman retraced her steps, silently returning to the waiting chandelier. She ascended the rope with astonishing agility, vanishing into the shadows above.

Once the figure had disappeared, the chandelier began to rise slowly, the screws effortlessly returning to their rightful place. It was as if the entire scene had unfolded without leaving a trace.

Back in the security room, Dave's eyelids grew heavy as sleep claimed him. Unbeknownst to him, his coffee had been tampered with, the unknown thief had spiked it with sleeping pills. The guard in the restroom, Mike, found himself occupied with an unexpected bout of gastrointestinal distress, courtesy of the laxative-laden coffee he had consumed.

As the storm raged outside, the mysterious thief slipped away, undetected, with the valuable Guarneri Violin, leaving behind a museum shrouded in darkness and secrets.

Little did Mike and Dave know that their seemingly mundane night shift would become a chapter in the legendary heist of the Pigeon Forge Museum, forever entwined with the haunting tales and the mysterious figure who danced through the shadows like a phantom in the storm.

The stormy night raged on, rain pouring relentlessly from the ink-black sky. Thunder roared and lightning cracked across the heavens, illuminating the city in brief, eerie flashes. Undeterred by the chaotic weather, the mysterious black figure darted through the darkness, her movements fluid and calculated.

From one rooftop to another, she leaped with astonishing grace and agility. The storm and the rain seemed inconsequential, unable to hinder her parkour prowess. It was as if she defied the laws of science and reality, becoming a creature of the night—a cat, a monkey, a force unto herself.

As the figure landed silently on the rooftop of an old apartment building, rainwater cascading off her sleek form, she scanned the surroundings. The dimly lit alley below beckoned, and she descended effortlessly, using the fire escape with practiced ease.

Waiting in the shadows was a sleek Porsche, its obsidian exterior blending seamlessly with the night. The figure approached the vehicle, her movements fluid and deliberate. She slid into the driver's seat, the car's interior enveloping her in warmth and luxury.

Samantha removed her mask and skilfully shed her all-black attire, revealing a sharp and sophisticated ensemble beneath. Her attorney clothes appeared immaculate, as if freshly pressed, despite the tumultuous night.

In the rear-view mirror, Samantha caught a glimpse of herself and paused for a moment to adjust her hair, ensuring it was perfectly in place. Satisfied with her appearance, she turned the ignition, the engine purred to life, and 'Shock the Monkey' by Pete Gabriel started playing in the car.

"Cover me when I run…

Cover me through the fire…

Something knocked me out the trees…

Now I'm on my knees…

Cover me, don't you monkey with the monkey…

Monkey, monkey, monkey…

Don't you know you're going to shock the monkey…"

A smirk crept across her face, the culmination of her audacious feat. It was a smirk that quickly transformed into maniacal laughter, a blend of triumph, adrenaline, and an insatiable thirst for the thrill.

Samantha was a woman of striking appearance. Standing tall with a slim figure, her presence commanded attention. Her blonde hair, styled in a shoulder-length cut, cascaded in loose waves that framed her face with elegance. The stormy night accentuated the intensity of her piercing eyes, which held a captivating allure.

Her features were meticulously crafted, exuding both sensuality and strength. A small nose, delicately sculpted, complemented her facial structure, adding a touch of refinement to her overall visage. But it was the mole positioned just above her lips that lent an intriguing quality to her beauty. With every smile or smirk, it seemed to accentuate her seductive charm, drawing others into her orbit.

With the priceless Guarneri Violin safely tucked in the backseat, securely fastened, Samantha navigated the rain-soaked streets with ease. The city lights blurred into a kaleidoscope of colors as she sped into the night, her destination clear in her mind.

Soon, Samantha arrived at the LAPD police department, its imposing structure standing tall amidst the chaos of the storm. Parking the Porsche in the precinct's lot, she knew that the violin, hidden in the back of the District Attorney's car, would be safe. No one would suspect that the instrument of immeasurable value was within reach.

Katz was suspicious of her and she had to be more careful than ever. She had to go home but not without stopping at the precinct to keep her story true in case Katz had any bright ideas. She had left precinct for a mere hour and she was secretly excited and thrilled at the little time she took to achieve such a feat of thievery.

Entering the precinct, Samantha exuded an air of authority, her mere presence commanding attention. The bustling officers and detectives paused momentarily, their focus sharpening at the sight of the esteemed District Attorney. It was as if time slowed for a brief moment, their gazes fixated on her before they resumed their duties, energized and determined.

Samantha's allure lay not only in her physical attributes but also in her confident demeanor. There was an air of dominance about her, an unspoken power that emanated from within. She carried herself with poise and grace, a woman who knew her worth and had no qualms about asserting herself.

Feminine yet formidable, Samantha was an embodiment of strength and allure. Her appearance was captivating, drawing both admiration and curiosity from those who crossed her path. Whether in the shadows of the night or the well-lit halls of power, she left an indelible impression, a woman whose presence demanded attention and respect.

Navigating through the precinct, Samantha nodded in acknowledgment to those she passed, a slight smile dancing on her lips. She made her way to the detective division office, closing the door behind her, shutting out the noise of the busy environment. A sense of calm washed over her as she sank into a comfortable chair, finally able to breathe.

Samantha's mind raced with exhilaration, the thrill of her daring escapade still coursing through her veins. She relished in the knowledge that she had accomplished the unthinkable, outwitting security measures and taking possession of the coveted Guarneri Violin.

As she leaned back in her chair, a mixture of satisfaction and anticipation filled her. The stolen violin held a value far beyond its monetary worth—it was a symbol of her audacity, her cunning, and her ability to navigate the shadows undetected.

With a contented sigh, Samantha took a moment to savor her triumph. A smile played upon her lips, hinting at the possibilities that lay ahead. She knew that her actions would reverberate through the city, forever altering the course of events. And as she sat in her office, basking in the thrill of her accomplishment, Samantha eagerly awaited the next chapter in her twisted tale of shadows and secrets.

She was not always this strong and accomplished. Samantha's childhood was marred by turmoil and abandonment, leaving lasting scars on her young soul. At the tender age of five, she found herself in the care of her aunt and uncle, having been abandoned by her own father, a man consumed by his vices and devoid of any sense of responsibility. His decision to walk out on his own flesh and blood branded him a heartless bastard in Samantha's eyes.

Samantha's mother was seeking a better future with someone else and shortly after her mother's departure, Samantha's father made a not-so-difficult choice to give her up to her uncle. It was a painful separation, as Samantha watched her father leave, hoping for an easier life without his child. Left in the care of her uncle, she was thrust into a new family dynamic that was meant to provide love and stability.

Although Samantha's new parents showered her with affection and care, she never truly connected with them. The wounds of her early abandonment ran deep, making it difficult for her to trust and form genuine bonds. As adolescence dawned, Samantha's restlessness grew, and she felt an insatiable desire for independence and freedom.

Unable to find solace within the confines of her adoptive home, Samantha began to rebel. Sneaking out became a regular occurrence as soon as she reached her teenage years. Escaping the clutches of the family she could never truly embrace, she made the daring decision to run away from home, leaving behind the safety and stability that her new parents had tried to provide.

Cutting ties with her past, Samantha embarked on a nomadic existence, drifting from one orphanage to another. It was a life fraught with uncertainty and constant upheaval. With each new placement, Samantha felt a sense of detachment, never fully belonging or feeling at ease. The instability of her circumstances fuelled her desire for something more, igniting dreams of grandeur within her heart.

Driven by her ambition, Samantha resorted to hustling and cheating, employing whatever means necessary to rise above her circumstances. Her thirst for success led her down a treacherous path, involving herself in thefts and robberies that allowed her to amass wealth and power. She discovered a knack for manipulation, honing her skills in the art of deception to secure her place in the criminal underworld.

In a twist of fate, Samantha managed to infiltrate the law, using her cunning and resourcefulness to navigate the system. Rising through the ranks and making important connections, she achieved the prestigious position of District Attorney, a position that granted her a semblance of authority and control. However, her involvement in criminal activities continued, fuelling her addiction to the thrill of the heist and the charm of valuable possessions.

Yet, as Samantha's crimes escalated, so did her descent into darkness. The lines between theft and violence blurred, and she found herself resorting to murder to protect her secrets and maintain her grip on power. Her obsession with control and dominance grew, consuming her every thought and action.

Samantha had become a twisted reflection of her troubled past, a complex and deeply flawed individual driven by a mix of resentment, ambition, and a distorted sense of justice. Her journey from a forsaken child to a ruthless criminal was a testament to the scars that never truly healed and the choices she made along the way.

Samantha's gaze remained fixed on the phone that sat before her, anticipation and urgency etched across her face.

Her office was dimly lit, with thunder and lightning casting shadows that danced on the walls as she anxiously awaited a call. Finally, the phone erupted into a series of shrill rings, breaking the silence that engulfed the room.

With a swift motion, Samantha reached out and answered the call, her voice steady and composed. The voice on the other end relayed the news she had been anticipating — a daring robbery had taken place at the esteemed Pigeon Forge Museum, and a priceless violin had been stolen. The weight of the situation hung heavily in the air as she absorbed the gravity of the crime.

Acknowledging the urgency of the matter, Samantha assured the caller that she would handle the situation. She ended the call with a decisive click and placed the phone back on the table, her mind already racing with thoughts and plans. She smiled to herself knowing the cat-and-mouse game that she was playing with LAPD.

As she sat there smiling, her eyes fell on the phone once again. With mischievousness in her eyes, she seized the phone and dialed a number, her fingers dancing across the keypad with practiced precision. The phone rang on the other end, and after a brief pause, a voice greeted her.

"Ian! We've got a situation," Samantha's voice crackled with a mix of urgency and authority in reply. Her words hung in the air, conveying the gravity of the situation to Detective Ian on the other end of the line. Ian immediately recognized the tone in her voice and understood the gravity of the situation.

"I am on my way, Chief," he said as he grabbed his coat and went out the door, this time knowing that Samantha has everything to do with this case but he will not be played by her anymore.

Chapter 13

Detective Ian sat at the worn-out table in the dimly lit room, frustration etched across his face. Across from him sat Katz who seemed shaken by Ian's accusations toward Samantha.

"I'm telling you, Mr. Katz, Samantha is up to something. I've been gathering evidence, but I just can't seem to convince you," Ian said, his voice filled with exasperation.

"Mr. Fisk, as much as I respect you I am sorry to say that you have lost your mind. My wife is not a criminal. She is the D.A. for crying out loud. There is nothing in the world that she does not have. I have spared no expense in taking care of her and you are saying that she is a criminal?" Katz asked leaning forward.

"I am not saying she is doing this for monetary gain. She is doing this because it is in her genes. She is following her father's path! She is protecting him!" Ian said softly.

"Mr. Katz, would you like some coffee?" Roni asked.

Katz nodded, "Yes, please, but no sugar. I'm diabetic."

As Roni poured the coffee, Katz began to open up, "You know, I suspected something was off with Samantha. She'd come home late, acting all suspicious. But I never imagined she was involved in criminal activities."

Roni exchanged a glance with Ian before she spoke, "That's not all, Katz. Samantha is the daughter of the notorious criminal, Samuel Grundfeld. She never mentioned this crucial piece of information to us. It makes her a prime suspect, and we think she might be protecting her father."

Katz looked visibly worried as he gazed at the table, his mind racing. "What help do you need from me?" he asked, finally looking up at Ian.

Ian leaned forward, his tone serious, "We need to tap Samantha's phone, and you need to wear a wire so we can monitor her conversations. It's the only way we can find out what she's up to."

Roni handed Katz a small button-sized device and a wire. "Stick this under the telephone on her desk at home," she instructed.

Katz held the tiny device in his hand, hesitating for a moment before nodding. "If Samantha is innocent, we'll know, and we'll keep her out of the investigation without her knowing you've helped us," Ian assured him.

With a worried expression, Katz understood the gravity of the situation. "We need to act fast. If Samantha is indeed involved in criminal activities, my life could be at stake," he admitted.

As the plan started to take shape, the room was filled with an air of urgency. Time was of the essence, and Katz knew that the fate of his family and possibly his own life hung in the balance.

Katz left the room shaking Ian's hand and with a morbid look on his face.

Ian slammed his fist on the table, "Mother f..." the sound reverberating through the room.

Roni placed a comforting hand on Ian's shoulder who looked like he was at the end of his wit.

"Damn it! That bitch is making a fool out of everyone! She's been playing with us all along Roni. We need to bring her in before she does any more damage or before Katz breaks" Ian said in anger.

"Chief, I understand your concerns, but rushing into this might do more harm than good. We don't have any solid evidence against Samantha" Roni said sitting across Ian.

Ian sighed, his frustration momentarily giving way to a sense of resignation. "You're right, Roni. We can't risk our reputations without concrete proof. But I hope Katz was wise enough not to disclose my name. If Samantha finds out I've been investigating her, both of us could be her next victims."

Roni nodded, understanding the gravity of the situation. "We need to be cautious, Chief. Samantha is cunning, and she knows how to manipulate situations to her advantage. We have to play this smart."

Ian's gaze hardened, determination gleaming in his eyes. "We will, Roni. We'll find a way to bring her to justice, but we must tread carefully. If Katz does as he is told we will know what she is up to in a couple of days. We gotta be patient"

Curiosity getting the better of her, Roni asked, "They have been married for ten years. Did Katz have any idea about her criminal activities when you went to see him in his office?"

Ian's frustration resurfaced as he recounted the encounter. "He denied everything, Roni. He acted as if I was accusing an innocent woman."

Roni furrowed her brow. "That's unsettling. Do you think Samantha has something on him, something that makes him protect her at all costs?"

Ian leaned forward, his voice laced with grim determination. "I do think so. But I may have struck a chord in him. When I mentioned Simon and that he is currently serving time in prison, he looked visibly stunned. If he's a wise man, he'll keep a close eye on Samantha."

Roni nodded, absorbing Ian's words. As they sat in that dimly lit room, Ian knew that they had a formidable opponent in Samantha, but he was willing to wait, biding his time until the truth unraveled. He couldn't help but feel a sense of urgency, though, for with each passing day, Samantha's web of deception tightened around their lives.

As Ian and Roni dived deeper into the mind of Samantha they figured out an important point. It was not her fault. The way she was. Samantha's life had been marred by a series of unfortunate events, starting from the very foundation of her existence. She was born into a broken family, where love and stability were scarce commodities. Her mother, consumed by her own desires, abandoned Samantha at a tender age for another man. The betrayal was etched deep into Samantha's young heart, leaving her feeling unwanted and abandoned.

Her father, Samuel, was equally culpable in this shattered family dynamic. He failed to take responsibility for Samantha, leaving her adrift in a sea of uncertainty. But what scarred Samantha, even more, was the toxic environment she witnessed between her parents. Their relationship was marred by infidelity and abuse, the kind no child should ever bear witness to.

As the years passed, Samantha's emotional well-being suffered greatly from the absence of a stable family unit. It was a void that couldn't be filled, no matter how hard she tried. When she was just a child, fate intervened in the form of Simon who saw his own daughter in the broken girl. Simon, who had no child of his own, took Samantha under his wing and adopted her.

However, despite Simon's best intentions, Samantha never truly felt a connection to him. Resentment and anger swirled within her, fueled by the deep-rooted pain of her past. She despised Simon, blaming him for her fractured childhood and the absence of her biological father, Samuel.

"You look like him! You are nothing like him!" Simon's words echoed in Ian's ears.

The resentment grew stronger when Samantha was only ten years old and Simon found himself behind bars, imprisoned for a crime that shook the foundation of their fragile family. The news shattered what little semblance of stability Samantha had left, further intensifying her feelings of anger and abandonment.

Samantha's turbulent upbringing and the void left by her father's absence took a toll on her young and impressionable mind. She grew up in a harsh and unforgiving world, where survival became her sole purpose. Bouncing from one foster home to another, and from orphanage to orphanage, Samantha experienced the harsh realities of life in all their rawness.

The scars of her past etched themselves into her psyche, leaving an indelible mark on her soul. She became hardened, a product of the pain and suffering she endured. The world had been cruel to her, and she saw no reason to show it any kindness in return.

As Samantha blossomed into womanhood, she chose to embrace the darkness within her. She no longer sought solace or redemption; instead, she sought vengeance. The legacy of her biological father, Samuel, loomed over her like a malevolent specter, whispering in her ear, urging her to inflict the same suffering she had endured.

Samantha reconnected with her father after a long search for him and when she found him she felt she was like him in more ways than she ever imagined. Forgetting the past she learned the art of deception and manipulation from Samuel and he taught her every trick in his book to make her one of the most elusive and cunning criminals in history.

Honing her new skills, in her pursuit of reckless goals, Samantha turned to a life of crime, becoming a cold and ruthless predator. Robbery and murder became her twisted tools of retribution, as she exacted her own form of justice as a D.A. on those she deemed deserving. The pain she inflicted upon others was an embodiment of the pain that had consumed her own life.

Samantha's actions were not merely driven by greed or a lust for power; they were borne out of a deep-seated need to replicate the suffering she had endured. The broken pieces of her past had shaped her into a woman who knew no bounds, who saw the world through a distorted lens of pain and vengeance.

As Samantha continued down this dark path, her actions became increasingly brazen and audacious. The world looked upon her with fear and fascination, unaware of the tumultuous journey that had brought her to this point. She was a living embodiment of the consequences of a fractured childhood, a testament to the devastating impact of a broken family.

Little did Samantha know that her path would soon intersect with those who were determined to bring her to justice, Ian and Roni. They were driven by a desire to protect and uphold the law. They were closing in on her and she could feel it on her neck. But as they delved deeper into Samantha's past, they came to realize that her story was not one of pure villainy, but rather a tragic tale of a lost soul consumed by the legacy of her broken family.

Chapter 14

Ian and Roni sat across Samantha, their eyes locked in a silent exchange of energies.

"Any updates on the violin theft case Detectives?" Samantha asked in her usual tone breaking the silence.

"Not yet boss" Ian replied, his voice steady and assured.

"But I've recently made contact with someone who might possess valuable information on the criminal. We're closing in, and I can promise you this – we'll have great news for you in a couple of days."

Samantha had a wild look in her eyes that could easily be concealed from a person who was intimidated by her. Ian knowing who she was pretending to be, made her look like a criminal to him so he was fearless staring in her eyes as she looked away and took a deep breath, exhaling a plume of smoke from her cigarette, a small act of solace in the midst of uncertainty.

"I trust you, Ian," she said, her voice laced with confidence. "Roni and you are the best detectives the LAPD offers. I believe in your abilities to solve this case."

Ian nodded appreciatively, acknowledging Samantha's faith in their skills.

"Thank you, Samantha," Roni chimed in. "We won't rest until we've uncovered the truth and brought this clown to justice. You have our word."

Samantha's gaze shifted between Ian and Roni, the gravity of their commitment mirrored in her expression.

As they prepared to part ways, Samantha stubbed out her cigarette, a symbol of her trust in their abilities. "I'll be waiting eagerly for the good news," she said.

Ian and Roni rose from their seats, their minds already racing with strategies and leads. They shared a brief nod, a silent affirmation of their shared determination to uncover the truth.

"Rest assured, Samantha," Ian said, his voice filled with conviction. "We won't let you down."

With that, they bid farewell to Samantha. The case had become personal – a quest to restore the trust of the people in LAPD.

As they left the room, Ian couldn't help but feel the weight of his professional ego weighing heavily on his shoulders. The words of 'reassurance' he had offered Samantha were not merely empty promises – they were a testament that they were going to catch her and had made that claim in her face.

Roni chuckled as she navigated the winding roads, her trust in Ian unwavering. "Wow, you could cut the tension in the room with a knife," she remarked, recalling the charged atmosphere in Samantha's cabin.

Ian nodded, his mind consumed with thoughts of the investigation. "Yes, and I have a feeling Samantha suspects that we've spoken to her husband," he replied, his tone filled with certainty.

Roni glanced at Ian, her curiosity piqued. "You deliberately hinted at our progress in the case, didn't you? To gauge her reaction?"

Ian grinned, a mischievous glint in his eyes. "Exactly, Roni. I wanted to observe any changes in her behavior towards us."

Roni's grip tightened on the steering wheel, her focus shifting between the road ahead and Ian's words. "And what did you observe?" she inquired, eager for any insights that could aid their investigation.

Ian leaned back in his seat, contemplating his observations. "Samantha is a master at concealing her emotions, but she couldn't hide a subtle moment of anxiety when I mentioned my confidence in having found the culprit. She looked away, just for a moment."

Roni nodded a mixture of frustration and determination etched on her face. "It's not enough to bring her to justice," she mused, her voice tinged with disappointment.

Ian's gaze shifted to Roni, his expression confident and resolute. "No, it's not enough yet. But now that she believes we're onto her, she'll become more cautious. We just need to monitor her closely and religiously. Trust me, Roni, she'll slip up eventually."

Roni met Ian's gaze, the weight of their shared mission settling between them. With a blank tone, she affirmed her trust in him. "Religiously? Got it. I trust you, Chief. Take me to church."

Ian burst into laughter, the tension momentarily broken. "Attaboy, Roni," he exclaimed, his laughter echoing through the car. They drove on, their determination fortified, as they headed towards their next destination, ready to uncover the truth and bring Samantha to justice.

Roni and Ian sat in tense anticipation inside the car parked outside Samantha's house. It had been days of surveillance, waiting for the moment when Samantha would unknowingly reveal herself. Ian was certain of Samantha's guilt, convinced she was responsible for the murders that had plagued the city.

Roni asked Ian, "What's the update on Katz?" Ian replied, "You would not believe me. I kept calling him, and he did not pick up, so I thought maybe he got weak and ratted us out to Samantha. But just when I was losing hope, I got a call from him."

Roni's interest grew, and she eagerly urged Ian to continue. Ian went on, saying, "He called me and told me that he has placed the listening device's transmitter under Samantha's desk phone. He's even wearing a wire so that we can listen to what Samantha is doing, even when he's fast asleep. Katz mentioned that he didn't want to come on a call with me because he was worried that Samantha might have tapped his phone. That's why he called me from a payphone."

Impressed, Roni nodded and remarked, "Not bad, Katz is not as dumb as he looks, but it has been almost a week, Chief. When is she going to slip up?"

Ian's eyes flickered with determination as he adjusted the listening device.

"F'n piece... of... shi..." A distorted voice crackled through the receiver, catching their attention.

"Today is the day," Ian whispered, a surge of excitement coursing through him. Roni's eyes widened in surprise, mirroring his sentiment.

"Ok Detective Ian, I hope you hear me. I am all set, it is 2:00 a.m. and Samantha is still out, the transmitter is in place and you can also listen to what she says to me through this wire... I hope. Here goes nothing" Katz's voice came through the receiver before the receiver went silent again.

It was not long before Samantha's car appeared in their line of sight. They leaned in their ears attuned to the growing sound of the incoming vehicle.

As her car crossed theirs, the familiar voice of Johnny Cash filled the airwaves, playing from her car radio. The lyrics of the song resonated with irony and significance.

"When I was just a baby my mama told me

Son, always be a good boy, don't ever play with guns

But I shot a man in Reno just to watch him die

When I hear that whistle blowing, I hang my head and cry"

Ian looked at Roni, a smirk playing on his lips. "Music tells you a lot about a person, eh?"

Roni couldn't help but chuckle softly at the ironic choice of song. They continued to listen intently as Samantha parked her car in the garage, their focus honed on capturing any potential clues.

The faint sounds of the car gate opening and closing reached their ears through the wire Katz was wearing. Samantha's movements within her house became audible as she opened her fridge and retrieved a beer, the distinctive sound of its opening resonating through the air.

Ian and Roni exchanged a knowing look, realizing that Samantha was about to relax in her study, likely believing she was safe from prying eyes and ears. Katz was waiting for her in their shared study and as she entered the study, she hugged Katz from behind, asking, "Why are you still up, Will?"

Katz replied sarcastically, "Why were you out so late, Samantha?"

Though slightly taken aback by his response, Samantha frowned behind his back but couldn't help but chuckle. "We've been over this so many times, baby. Come, let me get you a cup of coffee, and then we can both go to sleep," she suggested, trying to ease the tension between them.

Unbeknownst to Samantha, Ian, and Roni were listening. They heard him reluctantly agree to her offer, his tone somewhat softened. As the night wore on, Samantha continued to be awfully nice to Katz, chatting with him about their day and making sure he was comfortable before they retired to bed.

Ian and Roni were surprised by Samantha's demeanor; she seemed genuinely caring and affectionate towards Katz, making them question whether she was truly involved in the criminal activities they suspected.

Once they were in bed, Roni and Ian heard Katz's loud snoring through the listening device. They exchanged glances, perplexed by the situation.

"Either Katz is a great actor, or he doesn't give a rat's ass about this operation," Roni whispered to Ian. "Who in their right mind can sleep so peacefully while wearing a wire?"

Ian furrowed his brows, deep in thought, and then mused, "Maybe Samantha has drugged him. It's possible."

The detectives were left with more questions than answers, and they knew they needed to tread carefully. While the conversation shed some light on Katz's behavior, it also raised doubts about Samantha's true intentions.

An hour passed with no significant developments. Frustration started to seep in as they feared another failed attempt at gathering evidence. "Will? Oh, Will?" Samantha's voice cooed through the speakers followed by rustling of the bed sheet and clothes.

"She's checking if he is asleep!" Roni said her eyes open wide in realization.

"Ugh, why do I have to do this every single f'n day? No worries. It is only a matter of days when I will finally get rid of you and that old bastard. I know just the right things to put in a delicious meal to send you on your way" Samantha's voice was dripping poison. She was talking to her husband while he slept. Ian and Roni were slightly surprised to hear a glimpse of her true personality.

They heard loud footsteps walking away from Katz and going towards the study. Their attention was instantly captured as they heard the approaching footsteps and the creaking of a door opening.

Samantha sighed and the sound of a lighter clicking followed by a deep inhale could be heard clearly. She was cursing under her breath when she picked up the phone and dialed a number. After dialing a couple of times, the person on the other side picked up. The sounds of Samantha's conversation came through the earpieces, filled with tension and anger.

"Samuel, it's me, Samantha. Why the hell did it take you so long to pick up the goddamn phone? I pay for all your shit and you just have to do one thing and you cannot even do that!" Samantha said over the phone in an angry tone.

"She sounds furious," Roni said in a whisper.

"I can't believe she's talking to her own father like that," Ian said gritting his teeth.

"What? You ran out? It has only been a week and you have already spent it? No! I won't give you any more money! You've squandered enough of it already. Do you think I'll keep funding your lifestyle while I have a bullseye on my back? Think again old man" she said foaming at her mouth.

Ian and Roni exchange a look of astonishment.

"She's cutting him off. She's had enough of his schemes. She thinks he is just a weak link now" Ian said his grip tightening on the steering wheel.

"I am going to gut you like a pig Samuel," Samantha said in a booming voice.

"We need to be careful. Samantha's capable of anything," Ian said firmly.

They continued listening intently as Samantha's voice grows colder.

"No! You listen to me! We are going to do this my way or I will add your name to the obituary Logan Johnson," Samantha said in a low and menacing voice. "I will come to see you next week with your new identity 'Thomas Stevens' and some money to last you till you are dead! Now scram," she added before she hung up.

Ian glanced at Roni, concern etched on her face.

"This isn't going to end well. Samantha is cutting ties, and her father won't take it lightly," Roni said.

"I hope he does not hold back," Ian said smiling.

"We got her Chief!" Roni said balling her fist in triumph. "This is evidence! We can get a proper investigation started on her based on this," she added.

"Would not you rather catch the monkey red-handed though?" Ian said turning and facing Roni.

"I don't understand," Roni said confused.

"Ah! I love this part! It is time for a master class Roni, watch and learn" Ian said excitedly, his eye filled with the thrill of the chase.

Roni was slightly uncomfortable with the sudden spike in the energy inside the car.

"What does it mean!"

Ian turned the ignition on and started revving the car.

"It means buckle up Dorothy because Kansas is going bye-bye," Ian said as he put the car in gear and sped off spinning his own web around Samantha.

A cold, foggy Friday night enveloped Samantha's home, shrouding it in an eerie stillness. Her husband Katz, lay in a deep slumber, blissfully unaware of the world around him, courtesy of the sleeping pills Samantha had administered as part of her routine. However, this particular night, she had increased the dosage, intentionally creating a concoction that put Katz to sleep for enough time for Samantha to get done with Samuel without Katz suspecting her.

Within the confines of her study, Samantha stood, phone pressed to her ear, engaged in a cryptic conversation with Samuel. The urgency in her voice was palpable as she reassured him, "Calm down okay? I will do whatever you say. I am sorry Father. I have the money now. You don't need to do this."

As she concluded the call, a surge of frustration coursed through her veins, and she unleashed a torrent of profanities at an invisible person in front of her, venting her anger and desperation.

Gathering her resolve, Samantha swiftly proceeded to her bedroom, her footsteps silent in the dimly lit hallway. In a meticulous display of efficiency, she retrieved all the cash and jewellery stashed away in the guest room.

Clutching her newfound treasures tightly in a duffle bag, she emerged into the night, stepping into her sleek black car, a vehicle as enigmatic as its owner.

Before embarking on her voyage, Samantha glanced at her reflection in the rearview mirror a hundred times, seeking reassurance and perfection in her facade.

Satisfied, she finally set her sights on the highway and accelerated into the unknown, driving relentlessly through the night.

This plan was her grandest yet, a convergence of hidden objectives and a need of the moment—a means to kill two birds with one strike.

For twenty-four uninterrupted hours, Samantha navigated the roads, her resolve unwavering. She made occasional stops for sustenance and brief naps, fueling herself with determination and a calculated sense of urgency. She arrived in South Dakota at the exact time she had departed from her home as if time itself conspired to maintain the equilibrium of her mysterious endeavor.

She drove to a shady little motel on the outskirts of the city. Seeking refuge in the shadowy and dubious motel, Samantha approached the receptionist with an air of magnetic allure. With a gaze that betrayed his fascination, the receptionist ogled her sultry presence, instantly entranced.

Hiding her true identity, Samantha claimed her reservation, stating, "I made a booking under the name of Mrs. Jameson."

As the receptionist handed her the key, his infatuated gaze lingered, captivated by her enigmatic charm. She accepted the key with a knowing smile, concealing her true intentions beneath her carefully crafted facade. Making her way to her motel room, Samantha closed the door behind her.

In a ritualistic manner, she prepared herself for what lay ahead. The warm water cascaded over her body, cleansing her spirit and instilling a sense of rejuvenation. Dressed in a skin-clad black bodysuit that clung to her every curve, Samantha felt a surge of power coursing through her veins. Cloaking herself in a luxurious leather jacket, she regarded her reflection in the mirror, a vision of determination and purpose. A woman on a mission.

With a swift motion, Samantha locked the door behind her, sealing her fate. Unperturbed, she casually leaped out of the window, her movements fluid and effortless. Stealthily, she navigated her way to the rear of the motel, where an inconspicuous motorcycle awaited her arrival, hidden from prying eyes.

Mounting the sleek machine, Samantha melded with the night, her purpose concealed in the darkness. The engine roared to life, its ominous growl resonating through the silent air. With unwavering determination, she accelerated into the abyss, embarking on her enigmatic journey, where shadows whispered secrets and destiny awaited its unveiling.

Samuel A.K.A Logan Johnson soon-to-be Thomas Stevens anxiously awaited in the dimly lit confines of his garage, his senses heightened in anticipation. Suddenly, he heard it—a faint hum resonating through the air. The sound grew louder, drawing closer with each passing moment until it came to a halt just outside the door. His heart pounded within his chest as he prepared himself for what awaited on the other side.

A light, playful knock echoed through the garage, sending chills down Logan's spine. The circumstances gave the innocent gesture an eerie edge. "Dad? You there? Daddy?" Samantha's voice cooed sweetly from behind the door, but the tone carried an unsettling quality. Trembling, Logan managed to respond, "It's open, honey. Come in."

The doorknob turned, and Samantha entered the room, her wide smile appearing unnervingly artificial. She carried a duffle bag, which she unzipped and threw in front of Logan. "Here! I got you all the money in the world Daddy! Is that all you wanted? Huh? Old bastard!" she spat, her words dripping with venom.

"That is no way to talk to your old man," Samuel replied, his tone blank and devoid of emotion.

"Huh? Listen, you little prick! You're out of prison because of me! I saved you from all the trouble all these years. Funding your gambling habits and your taste for women!" Samantha's voice grew louder, her anger building with every word.

"I don't owe you shit. I taught you what you know. Whoever you are, it's because of me!" Samuel retorted, his voice filled with anger.

"I learned it the hard way. I was on my own. You begged me for money. I didn't need your help. You reeled me in with your old man seeking redemption sob story and blackmailed me for money," Samantha's voice escalated, her frustration boiling over.

"No matter what you do, you can never be like me. I stole, but I never killed anyone. I'm not a killer, but an artist, and you can never be like me," Samuel stoked the flames, his words dripping with superiority.

"I don't want to be like you, you son of a bitch. I am not like you. A coward hiding in a hole after you get that cheese. I am a beast! I have killed! I am an apex predator, and nobody can stop me," Samantha declared, her voice filled with defiance.

She picked up the heavy duffle bag filled with jewelry and cash and pushed it against Samuel's chest.

"You're on your way to Ecuador under the name of Thomas Stevens. I am taking you to the airport in the morning to get you through the red tape. One more word out of you and you are a dead man! No one will look for you because you do not exist!" she said in a threatening and commanding tone.

Samuel, with grease on his face and hands dirty from a long day of work, looked at his daughter, Samantha, with tears welling up in his eyes. Despite his weariness, he replied, "OK, my darling daughter." He knew he had little choice but to comply with her demands.

"What about Will?" he asked, hoping for some reassurance. Samantha looked at him with a hint of coldness in her eyes and replied, "I will come to see you when he is taken care of. No need to worry." Her response sent shivers down Samuel's spine, realizing the gravity of the situation.

As Samantha spoke about Katz's health, Samuel's heart sank further. "Will is a diabetic with high blood pressure and high cholesterol, 75lbs overweight," she said, her voice chillingly calm. "I know what to put in his favorite dinner meal to allow him to slip into a diabetic coma within 90 minutes. Now let's go I do not have all night!"

Samuel was deeply troubled by his daughter's words, torn between his loyalty to his family and the dangerous path she was going down. He knew he had to be careful with every step he took, as the consequences of getting caught could be dire for both him and Katz. Samuel nodded before picking up the bags he had packed for his journey while Samantha lit up a cigarette while heading out the door saying "Pathetic".

Unbeknownst to Samantha, Ian, and Roni, who had been tirelessly investigating Samantha's criminal activities were surveilling from a distance, listening intently to every word through their concealed audio equipment and the person Samantha was talking to was not Samuel, but his twin brother Simon.

It was a part of Ian's ingenious plan. While Samantha was on the phone with Samuel telling him about her plans to send him to Ecuador with a new name and enough money to live until he was dead. Her conversation was being monitored by Ian and Roni, and it gave them a probable cause to go and arrest Samuel.

They got Simon out for 5 days after making arrangements with the assistant D.A. and the Warden and took him to South Dakota where they arrested Samuel and put Simon in his place.

Simon was told everything Samantha and Samuel were doing, saying, and plotting. They told him about their plan of arresting Samuel and disguising Simon as Samuel. Simon agreed to Ian's plan and now here he was holding a bag full of money and jewelry ready to go to the airport with Samantha.

After Simon told Samantha he was done packing, Samantha drove him to the airport in his car. She believed she was taking her father, Samuel, to escape the country as per their plan.

As they approached the airport, Samantha's heart raced with anticipation. She kept glancing at "Samuel," unaware of the switch. Simon, doing his best to imitate his brother's demeanor, maintained a stoic expression and occasionally nodded in response to Samantha's chatter.

Upon reaching the airport, Samantha parked the car and accompanied Simon to the check-in counter. She had meticulously prepared all the necessary documents for Samuel's (Simon's) smooth departure and due to her connections, she was able to get him through all the security checks with ease.

Samantha confidently handed over the passports and tickets, trying to appear composed despite her underlying nerves. The airport staff processed the documents, occasionally glancing at the two individuals. Simon did his best to mimic Samuel's behavior, but he couldn't help feeling guilty about deceiving Samantha. Nevertheless, he understood the urgency of the situation and the need to protect the people from Samantha's dangerous schemes.

As they made their way through the security checks, Samantha hugged "Samuel" tightly, whispering in his ear.

"My people in Ecuador will receive you and get you out safely. Do not ever come back. If you even look in L.A.'s direction again I am going to wipe you off the face of this earth like the shit stain you are" she said in Simon's ear with a smile on her face.

Simon was furious and felt a pang of sadness, knowing he couldn't reveal his true identity and jeopardize the plan.

Finally, they reached the departure gate, and Samantha watched as "Samuel" went inside and disappeared from her sight. She waved goodbye believing she had successfully sent her father away to safety.

Feeling a mix of relief and accomplishment, Samantha went back to the shady motel, checked out and headed back to Los Angeles, ready to focus on the next part of her plan. Little did she know that Samuel was locked up in a cell in L.A. ready to be interrogated by Ian and Roni.

Meanwhile, after Samantha left the airport, Ian and Roni, who had orchestrated the switch, quietly brought Simon back to Los Angeles. The stage was set for a high-stakes confrontation between Simon and Samuel.

Chapter 15

"Hi brother, long time," Simon said to Samuel as they stood face to face in the shock room. The moment was charged with emotions as Samuel looked at Simon, his expression resembling that of someone who had seen a ghost. Samuel's heart weighed heavy with regret, and he mustered the courage to say, "I am sorry I put you through this."

Simon, however, showed remarkable understanding and replied, "It's all right. I did what I had to do to protect you, and you did what you had to do. But now, you have to pay the price for your actions." Despite the gravity of the situation, Simon's tone remained composed, acknowledging the consequences of their choices.

Standing at a distance, Ian and Roni, watched as this once-in-a-lifetime moment unfolded before them. They were privy to the deep emotions and complicated history that had brought the two brothers to this point.

Simon and Samuel continued to exchange words, their conversation tinged with remorse and regret. Samuel repeatedly apologized, seeking forgiveness for the pain he had caused his brother. In response, Simon displayed a sense of acceptance and peace, as if coming to terms with the situation and finding closure in their interaction.

As Ian and Roni observed this exchange, they couldn't help but be moved by the profound bond between the two brothers, despite the difficult circumstances they found themselves in. In their line of work, they often dealt with the darker side of human nature, but witnessing this raw and genuine moment of reconciliation reminded them of the complexities and depths of human relationships.

The detectives knew that their role in this situation was not to interfere but to ensure justice prevailed. They had followed leads, gathered evidence, and finally brought the two brothers together in this crucial moment. It was now up to the legal system to take its course.

As Simon and Samuel continued their conversation, Simon, with a content look on his face, seemed to have found some measure of closure and understanding, while Samuel bore the burden of his actions, ready to face the consequences.

.

Ian intervened, cutting short Simon and Samuel's conversation, stating firmly, "Time for chit-chatting is over. I have to ask you some questions."

As the Correctional Officer, Robert, and Roni approached, they assisted Samuel to the chair in the shock room. Robert securely tied Samuel's hands and legs to the chair, reassuring him, "Don't worry, this is only going to hurt a lot."

Feeling desperate to prove his innocence, Samuel protested, "I am innocent. She set me up." However, Robert brushed off his claims, retorting, "Yeah, yeah, tell it to the judge."

Roni, concerned about Simon's involvement, suggested, "Simon, let's move you to your cell. You don't need to witness this." But Simon's eyes glinted with a wild intensity as he insisted, "No, I need to see it."

With a sense of trepidation, Roni exchanged a look with Ian, who stood poised at the control panel. After receiving an affirmative nod from Ian, the interrogation began. Ian addressed Samuel sternly, "Samuel Grundfeld, tell us about everything you have done from end to start."

"I already told you I am inn…" Before Samuel could complete his sentence, Ian pressed the button on the control panel, sending shock waves through Samuel's body, causing him to jolt and the chair to clank loudly. Simon, seemingly unaffected, observed the process without blinking, a peculiar satisfaction evident in his eyes.

Ian repeated the process two more times, each time prompting Samuel to writhe in discomfort. Under the physical strain and mental pressure, Samuel finally broke.

"Make it stop," Samuel said crying. He confessed to every detail of his involvement in the robberies and murders and how he had assisted Samantha the D.A. in becoming one of the most notorious criminals to exist.

As Samuel's confession unfolded, it became evident that the investigation had been relentless and the evidence overwhelming. Ian and Roni had been tenacious in their pursuit of the truth, and their efforts had culminated in this crucial moment. Despite the discomfort of the interrogation, they knew it was essential to extract the truth and hold the guilty accountable.

Simon's demeanor softened as he heard Samuel's confession, his wild look giving way to a mix of emotions. It was a difficult moment for him but Simon also understood that justice needed to be served, and this was the path they had to take.

With the confession recorded, Roni and Ian moved in toward the last phase of the plan to apprehend Samantha and ensure that justice was served. The plan was working, and it was now time to catch the monkey red-handed.

Chapter 16

"Now if there's a smile on my face

It's only there trying to fool the public

But when it comes down to fooling you

Now honey that's quite a different subject

But don't let my glad expression

Give you the wrong impression

Really I'm sad, oh, I'm sadder than sad

You're gone and I'm hurting so bad

Like a clown I appear to be glad (sad, sad, sad, sad)"

Samantha's jolly mood persisted as she continued to prepare a meal for William Katz, her beloved husband. The nostalgic melody of "Tears of a Clown" played softly in the background, setting an eerie contrast to the sinister plan she was about to execute. Today marked a significant step toward her freedom, and she was resolute in her decision.

With meticulous planning, Samantha checked and double-checked the ingredients she had used, ensuring they would send her husband straight to heaven, quite literally. Her heart was heavy with the weight of her actions, but she knew she had to go through with it.

"I can't deal with your shit any longer Will. It's time for both of us to find peace," Samantha muttered under her breath.

As she prepared the meal, she thought about Katz's deteriorating health condition. She knew he is diabetic with high blood pressure and cholesterol and could not handle the dangerous combination of ingredients she had used. Samantha, fueled by her desperation for freedom continued making the last meal for Katz without any hesitation.

Just as she finished setting up Katz's meal on the dining table, she looked at the clock and realized that William was about to come home.

Samantha hurriedly left the kitchen to get dressed. She was avoiding being present when her plan took effect. She wanted to be far away, out of sight, when it happened.

In the bathroom, she took a long shower, allowing the warm water to wash away her anxiety. As the water cascaded down her curvy but fit body, she took a deep breath and steadied her nerves.

Once she was dressed, Samantha composed a note for William, trying to maintain a facade of normalcy. She left the note on the dining table next to his meal, kissing it with her red lipstick to add a touch of affection.

The note read: "I am going to be home late, love. I have made food; it is set on the table. Please do not wait for me. I will be home soon. Love, Sam."

Before leaving the house, Samantha took a moment to compose herself, her heart racing as she faced the consequences of her actions. She stepped outside, inhaling deeply as if to brace herself for what was to come.

Finally, she got into her car, her hands trembling on the steering wheel not with worry but with excitement. The weight of her decision bore down on her, but she felt a glimmer of hope for the freedom she so desperately sought. This plan was as well thought as the other plans she had executed in the past flawlessly and there was no way she was getting caught.

Samantha's mind was a whirlwind of emotions as she drove to the nearby liquor store. Her heart pounded with anticipation, knowing that tonight would mark a turning point in her life. She parked her car and stepped into the store, her eyes scanning the shelves until she found what she was looking for—a bottle of Jameson, her drink of choice for the evening.

With the bottle securely in her hand, Samantha couldn't help but smile. Tonight, she would finally be free of William Katz, the man whose influence she had once used to climb the ladder of success in her professional career. But now, he was nothing more than a burden, a hindrance to her ambitions. She envisioned a future filled with endless possibilities, liberated from the shackles of his presence.

Back in her car, Samantha eagerly opened the bottle and took a big gulp, savoring the taste of the smooth whiskey. As the liquid burned down her throat, she felt a sense of liberation, as if the alcohol itself was washing away her past troubles.

Samantha was well aware of her position as the D.A., and she relished in the feeling of invincibility it gave her. No one dared to challenge her, and she did as she pleased without fear of consequences. She played the role of a law-abiding and law-enforcing officer, a facade that masked the darkness she hid within.

In secret, Samantha had utilized her powerful position to commit numerous crimes, manipulating the law to suit her desires. With William Katz and her supposed father Samuel out of her life, she felt like a cunning predator, ready to seize every opportunity that came her way.

Her sleek black Jaguar roared as she cruised through the streets, celebrating her impending freedom. The wind tousled her hair, and the music blared through the car's speakers, creating an atmosphere of triumph and euphoria.

With every mile she covered, Samantha's determination grew stronger. Tonight was just the beginning of her reign, and she knew she had the power to shape her destiny, unbound by the constraints of her past.

As she drove, the city lights illuminated her path, and the world seemed to bend to her will. Samantha was ready to embrace the darkness within her, willing to do whatever it took to fulfill her ambitions. With Katz and Samuel no longer holding her back, she was an unstoppable force, prepared to conquer all that lay ahead.

After driving to her office, Samantha walked inside with a sense of purpose. She made her way to her desk, sinking into her chair with a hint of anticipation. Retrieving a cigarette from her pocket, she lit it up, the smoke swirling around her as she took a long, satisfying drag. A mischievous smile crept across her face, reveling in the pride she felt for the plan she had so carefully orchestrated.

With her heart still racing from the thrill of her recent actions, Samantha glanced at the phone on her desk. It had been a few hours since she had left the house, and she knew she should be expecting a call, just as she always did after executing anything sinister. The anticipation only added to her excitement, fueling her desire to continue her dark endeavors.

As she waited patiently, her mind was already at work, planning her next move, and carefully selecting her next targets. The rush of power surged through her veins, making her feel invincible and untouchable.

Amid her contemplation of the next robbery she intended to orchestrate, the phone suddenly rang loudly, shattering the silence of the office. Samantha's face lit up with a wide grin as she glanced at the clock on the wall, confirming that it was 1:00 a.m.

She let the phone ring for a few seconds, savoring the moment before she picked it up. Composing herself, she cleared her throat and answered with a practiced calmness, "Hello?"

"Hello, is this Samantha Williams?" the voice on the phone spoke.

"Yes, this is she. What can I do for you?" Samantha asked.

"We're calling from the Angeles hospital. We received a 911 call from your husband's neighbor. Mr. Katz complained of chest pain and believed he was having a heart attack. We rushed him in, and I'm sorry to inform you that he's now in a diabetic coma. We don't have any prognosis at this time," said the hospital staff.

Samantha's heart raced as she heard the news. She tried to maintain a facade of concern, but beneath it, she couldn't help but feel a sense of satisfaction. Her plan had worked, and she could see her vision of freedom coming true.

"Oh my goodness! Thank you for informing me. I'm on my way right now. Please keep me updated on his condition," Samantha said feigning worry.

"Of course. We'll keep you informed. Please make your way here as soon as possible" hospital staff replied.

Samantha hung up the phone and took a moment to savor the moment. A subtle smile played on her lips as she realized her husband's health crisis played perfectly into her carefully crafted plan. Her mind swirled with a mix of emotions, knowing that her desired outcome was inching closer.

She took her time getting back into her car, relishing every moment of the journey. The drive to the hospital felt surreal as if she were floating on a cloud of triumph. She kept up the facade of concern, praying that she would have to identify her husband's body, all the while hiding the dark truth of her involvement.

Arriving at the hospital, Samantha's heart raced with a blend of anticipation and excitement. She stepped out of her car and walked through the hospital doors, her heels clicking on the polished floors.

As she approached the reception desk, she tried to steady her emotions, presenting a facade of worry and fear for her husband's well-being.

"I'm here for William Katz. I was told he was brought in earlier. Can you please update me on his condition?" she said in a concerned tone.

The receptionist checked the records and gave Samantha a somber look before speaking. "I'm sorry, ma'am. His condition is critical, and the doctors are still working on stabilizing him. You can wait in the waiting area, and we'll keep you informed"

Samantha nodded, doing her best to appear distraught. As she waited, her mind drifted back to the cunning plan she had executed. Deep down, she knew that her husband's fate had been sealed by her own hands.

"Samantha Williams?" a voice said.

Samantha who was acting like she was worried sick lifted her head up, "Yes?"

"Please follow me it is urgent," the nurse said.

Samantha got up and nodded before following her out of the waiting room. Her heart raced as the nurse led her to the room where William was supposed to be. Her mind was a whirlwind of emotions, uncertain of what was waiting for her on the other side of that door. She took a deep breath, trying to steady herself as she entered the room.

When she entered the room she was surprised to see Ian and Roni waiting for her. Samantha was shocked to see them there but she thought that someone from the department must have informed them after the 911 call so she stayed calm.

"Thank God you guys are here. Where is Will? Is he okay?" Samantha said with fake concern.

The moment seemed surreal as Katz suddenly emerged from behind Ian, his face contorted with anger and hurt. He wasted no time in voicing his feelings, accusing Samantha, "I am here, and thank God for them, or you would have killed me, you lying evil bitch!"

Samantha's face turned pale as she struggled to process Katz's words. "What the hell?" she stammered, shocked beyond belief.

Still trying to maintain her facade of innocence, Samantha responded to Katz, "Honey! I was worried! Thank God you are okay!"

But the wild look in Samantha's eyes betrayed her true emotions, and Katz saw right through her act.

"I do not know what they told you, but they are lying! This is a setup!" Samantha said in a desperate attempt to deny the accusations, her mind racing for a way to get out of this situation.

"I wish it was a setup, but I have heard it from my own ears, Samantha! I could not believe my ears too, but then my test reports further proved that you have been drugging me for so long so you can sneak out and murder people!? I do not even know who you are anymore! You scare and disgust me!" Katz said looking at her, his eyes red with rage.

Undeterred, Samantha took a step closer to Katz, her voice quivering as she tried to reason with him, "Hey Will, baby... listen to me..."

However, before she could continue, Ian intervened, positioning himself between Samantha and Katz.

"All right, Samantha, the gig is up. You are under arrest", he said firmly.

Samantha's facade crumbled, and she lashed out at Ian, trying to intimidate him by threatening his position.

"Detective! Stay within your limits! I will get you suspended!" she said defiantly.

Roni who was standing silently till now could not stop herself and stepped forward from behind Ian, delivering a devastating uppercut that sent Samantha flying through the air. It was clear that Roni had had enough of it.

"I never liked you!" she announced. "Apex predator, you said? You're just an overconfident dumb arrogant bitch," Roni added.

Stunned, Samantha slowly regained her senses, only to find Roni standing above her.

"You set me up!" Samantha said her eyes wide with shock.

As Samantha's world spun in a daze from the blow she received from Roni, she felt the cold metal of the handcuffs encircle her wrists. Her attempts to resist were futile, and she realized she was now under arrest.

Roni, with a mix of anger and disappointment in her eyes, recited Samantha's Miranda rights, her voice unwavering even in the midst of the chaotic situation.

"You have the right to remain silent. Anything you say can and will be used against you in a court of law. You have the right to speak to an attorney, and to have an attorney present during any questioning. Wow, ironic," said Roni in a somber tone cuffing Samantha.

Samantha, now fully cognizant of the gravity of her actions and the consequences she faced, remained silent. Her mind raced with regret and disbelief as she was led away, the weight of her crimes pressing heavily on her shoulders.

As she was taken into custody, Samantha knew that her once carefully constructed world of deception had crumbled. The power and control she had enjoyed had slipped through her fingers, leaving her exposed and vulnerable.

It was a bitter irony, indeed, that the very tactics she had used to manipulate and deceive others had now turned against her. Her reign of darkness had come to an end, and she was now left to face the consequences of her actions.

As Samantha was led away, her eyes locked briefly with Katz's, filled with a mix of anger, hurt, and disappointment. She had lost everything she held dear, all because of her insatiable hunger for power and control.

The sound of the Miranda rights being recited echoed in her mind, a haunting reminder of the choices she had made and the paths she had chosen.

At that moment, Samantha realized that her downfall had been her own making. The seeds of deceit and manipulation she had sowed had grown into a tangled web that ensnared her in its grip.

Samantha seethed with anger and frustration as she found herself in a cold, dimly lit cell after being taken into custody. To her surprise, Simon, whom she had mistaken for her father Samuel earlier, walked into the cell area. Seeing him, she couldn't hold back her rage.

"You deceitful bastard! You lied to me! You betrayed me!" she said shouting.

"Samantha, calm down. I am not your father Samuel. I am his brother, your uncle Simon" he said calmly.

Samantha's anger shifted to confusion, but she couldn't see past her fury to listen to Simon's words.

"I don't care who you are! You're all the same! You've ruined everything!" Samantha said, still yelling.

Simon remained composed, unshaken by her outburst. He felt no regret in helping Ian and Roni apprehend her, knowing she deserved to face the consequences of her actions.

"You brought this upon yourself, Samantha. No matter how many years I spent in jail for a crime I didn't commit, I am content knowing that you are not my biological daughter. I wouldn't even bother to piss on you if you were on fire," Simon said.

The coldness of Simon's words cut deep into Samantha, but she refused to show any vulnerability. Her heart pounded with anger and humiliation as she felt the weight of her crimes pressing down on her.

Simon turned to leave, leaving Samantha to her thoughts and emotions. As he walked away, he added one last remark with a hint of disdain, "May you have interesting times."

The cell door closed, leaving Samantha alone with her own turmoil. Her anger turned into frustration, and she began yelling and howling in frustration. But her voice was drowned in the cacophony of other inmates mocking and taunting her.

At that moment, Samantha felt a sense of despair and isolation, realizing the depths of her own darkness and the consequences of her actions. The reality of her downfall was all too real, and she was now faced with the harsh truth of her choices.

As she sat alone in her cell, surrounded by the mocking voices of others, Samantha couldn't help but feel the weight of her own downfall. Her once powerful and cunning facade had crumbled, leaving her exposed and vulnerable.

In the hushed atmosphere of the courtroom, Ian stood confidently before the judge and jury, ready to present his case. He cleared his throat and began, his voice commanding attention.

"Your Honor, esteemed members of the jury, I stand before you today to shed light on the intricate web of deceit, violence, and manipulation that surrounds the defendant, Samantha," Ian began, his gaze sweeping across the room. "During the course of our investigation, my partner Veronica and I uncovered a crucial piece of information that links Samantha to her father and his insidious demands for money."

Gasps rippled through the courtroom as the revelation hung in the air. Ian continued, his voice steady and determined. "We traced Samantha's father to a remote location in South Dakota, and it was there that we successfully apprehended him. Recognizing Samantha's propensity for violence, we devised a plan. We used her father as bait, coercing him to make phone calls to Samantha, issuing threats and demands."

The judge leaned forward, his attention fully captivated by Ian's words. "You see, Your Honor, we knew Samantha to be a ruthless killer, capable of unspeakable acts. So we waited, patiently, for her next move, knowing she would stop at nothing to obtain what she desired."

Whispers buzzed through the courtroom as the magnitude of the situation became apparent. Ian's eyes met the jurors' gaze as he continued his account of events. "And just as we anticipated, Samantha made the call. She contacted Samuel, her biological father and partner in crime, informing him that she was coming with the money and that she will help him flee the country by forging a new identity for him. It was a calculated move, and we were ready."

The judge nodded, acknowledging the significance of Ian's testimony. "Please continue, Mr. Fisk. The court is listening."

With a momentary pause, Ian continued, his voice filled with conviction. "Your Honor, members of the jury, based on the evidence we have gathered, Samantha's crimes extend far beyond the realm of mere financial gain. She stands accused of the premeditated and cold-blooded murders of seven innocent individuals including an attempt to murder the renowned businessman and Casino Owner, her husband, William Katz. The depths of her malevolence are unfathomable."

A heavy silence fell over the courtroom as Ian's words reverberated. The judge, seemingly absorbed in contemplation, studied the evidence before him. After a prolonged moment, he finally spoke, his voice resolute. "In light of the evidence presented and the gravity of Samantha's crimes, this court hereby sentences her to the ultimate penalty: death."

The room erupted into murmurs and gasps, the weight of the judgment permeating the air. Yet, amid the chaos, Samantha remained stoic, her expression a mask of inscrutability.

Turning his attention to Samuel, the judge addressed him sternly. "Samuel A.K.A Logan, you have been found guilty of your involvement in these criminal activities. For your crimes, this court sentences you to serve 20 years in prison."

Logan's face contorted with a mixture of regret and resignation as the weight of the verdict settled upon him. His gaze briefly met Samantha's, their connection steeped in a shared history of darkness and manipulation.

As the proceedings came to an end, the courtroom began to empty slowly, the echoes of justice and consequence reverberating through the hall. Simon, who had been mistakenly apprehended, was finally granted his freedom, a glimmer of light amidst the shadows.

Samantha, unmoved by the judgment, maintained her composure, a chilling presence in the midst of the courtroom's emotional turbulence. The truth had been unveiled, and justice had prevailed, but the depths of Samantha's psyche remained shrouded in mystery.

The court proceedings had finally come to an end, and Ian and Roni found themselves outside the courthouse, basking in the aftermath of justice served. It was there that they encountered Simon, a victim of Samantha and Samuel's manipulation and abuse.

"You finally caught the monkey!" Simon exclaimed with a grin, acknowledging their victory.

"Oh yes, we did," Roni responded, her laughter bubbling forth. The weight of the case lifted from their shoulders, leaving room for a moment of lightheartedness.

"Thanks for cooperating, Simon," Ian said, extending his gratitude. "No, thank you, Mr. Fisk. I thought I was going to rot in there forever," Simon replied, his relief palpable.

"I understand, Simon. With Samantha's deep-rooted connections in the LAPD and the soft spot you had for your brother, there was no way for you to escape on your own. We are glad we could help," Ian said, shaking Simon's hand firmly.

"Come by my house I will be happy to serve you coffee. Take care" Simon smiled, a newfound sense of freedom emanating from him as he walked away, leaving behind the shadows of his past. The weight of the world lifted, replaced by a glimmer of hope for a brighter future.

"This feels great!" Roni exclaimed, stretching her arms in jubilation.

"Doesn't it?" Ian replied, a glimmer of satisfaction in his eyes. He watched Simon's retreating figure, a mix of admiration and understanding in his gaze.

"That was a great uppercut, I must say," Ian complimented Roni, recalling the pivotal moment in the hospital.

"Haha, thanks, boss. Did you see her face?" Roni chuckled, remembering Samantha's shocked expression.

"Yeah, she looked absolutely stunned," Ian agreed, the memory eliciting a sense of triumph.

"Yeah, like a shocked monkey," Roni added, and they both burst into laughter, the tension of the case dissipating with each peal of mirth.

As they climbed into their car, ready to embark on new mysteries waiting to be unraveled, they shared a camaraderie forged through countless investigations. The thrill of the unknown beckoned them forward, fueled by the knowledge that justice had been served.

And so, Ian and Roni drove away, their laughter echoing into the distance, ready to face whatever enigma lay ahead, knowing that together they were an unstoppable force, dedicated to bringing truth to the shadows and ensuring that the scales of justice remained in balance.

"Climbing up on Solsbury Hill

I could see the city light

Wind was blowing, time stood still

Eagle flew out of the night

He was something to observe

Came in close, I heard a voice

Standing, stretching every nerve

I had to listen, had no choice

I did not believe the information

Just had to trust imagination

My heart going "Boom-boom-boom"

"Son," he said

"Grab your things, I've come to take you home"

Made in the USA
Las Vegas, NV
01 April 2025

12bebdb1-8d30-4229-9fa4-bd2d92f2b6caR01